author

Candy's WILD RIDE

The Candy Cane Girls, book 3

By Bonnie Engstrom

Published by Forget Me Not Romances, a division of Winged Publications

Copyright © 2017 by Bonnie Engstrom

All rights reserved. No part of this publication may be resold, reproduced, stored in a retrieval system, or transmitted in any form or by any means, electronic, mechanical, recording, or otherwise, without the prior written permission of the author. Piracy is illegal. Thank you for respecting the hard work of this author.

This is a work of fiction. All characters, names, dialogue, incidents, and places either are the product of the author's imagination or are used fictitiously. Any resemblance to actual events, locales, or people, living or dead, is entirely coincidental.

ISBN-13: 979-8-3302-5701-0

SPECIAL THANKS TO

The real Bill Lord for allowing me to use his name and appearance. He was also the motorcycle expert for this story. Although I have not seen it myself, I am told he has an entire garage full of motorcycles that he repairs and purchases, or trades parts for and with. Fascinating man and a real life hero. The Bill I know of does not have a son, so both Bill Junior and the Senior title are both fictional. May the real Bill Lord please stand up!

To a girl named Laurie who I met in the supermarket parking lot when she steered her red Mini Harley Softail Slim into a space. I knew immediately it was the bike Candy would ride in the story. I regret I didn't have the insight to take a photo of it, but I did find it online. Super cute and perfect for a young woman.

To Kerrie Benvenuti who took time and special effort to take photos of Rogers Gardens so both Candy and I could visualize our bearings. It had been a long time since I was there, so her help was invaluable. That part of the story couldn't have been written without her help.

My preschool director daughter, Dana, who I snuck into this story, as well as my son, Brian, the surfer who lives in Costa Rica. It was a joy to include them. Miss Lorrie is again included, but sorry there is no recipe from her this time. But, Pastor Steve and his lovely wife Patti made the wedding special. Their joy for each other and for the Lord is almost legendary.

Again, my wonderful and patient husband Dave, resident chef, who held dinner many evenings while I wrote and edited. The dogs ate before we did! Thank you, Dave. See now what you signed up for fifty-two years ago. Gosh, shrink and author, what a combo!

My publisher, Cynthia Hickey of Forget Me Not Romances who has been extremely patient. She is the gem who made this and my other books realities.

Nava, the Director of Marketing for Rogers Gardens who answered many questions for me and clued me in about the Farmhouse Restaurant that would be open by the time the story concludes.

Author Darlene Franklin for getting me started on a Candy Cane story. Although we never published together as we had planned, she inspired me.

God! Thank You for giving me the words to say. I prayed so many times for those, and You answered. Sometimes in spurts of sentences, sometimes in inspirational ideas, and many times in encouragement from others. Somehow You got me through the crazy idea of having so many Bills in this story. You truly were my savior for this book and will forever be my Savior for all time.

CANDY'S WILD RIDE

Dear Reader ~

I hope you will enjoy this series that tells the stories of women who are what I call super friends ~ friends who committed as teenagers to prayer and loyalty bound by a moniker. The Candy Cane Girls are a unique group of sister friends. I hope their stories will inspire other young women. They are Sisters of Promise, promises they made when young and promises they've kept for generations.

I am hoping to start an inspiration, a situation or a way to encourage young women, especially teen girls, to write their own stories. I have three teenage granddaughters who are bright and talented but as far as I know do not record their thoughts and experiences. I also pray for other teen girls of friends. It troubles me they are not writing about their lives and experiences. Please join me in praying for an upcoming of young women writers.

As you read through this series, and I hope you will, please note how each book tells a story about individual women, how each struggle with a personal situation and overcomes it. Some of the circumstances they encounter are destined by faith and fate; but all require belief and commitment to each other and to the faith of each. I hope you will read every story to see how Cindy deals with her new love's health issues, and Candy takes her fears into action, and Connie . . . well she has a problem that she overcomes with the help of sweet Jake, her 'problems solving' dog. Jake will appear in many following books. He was my running companion for many years – the dearest dog. But Lola and Happy Arthur are shining woofers in their own stories.

But wait until you get to Natalie and Melanie! They hold the keys to lasting friendship. Their stories are almost legendary.

All stories in the series can be read individually, but you will enjoy them more and understand them more if you read them in order.

Noelle, Cindy, Connie, Candy, Natalie, Doreen and especially Melanie will steal your heart.

You will have fun with the different wedding venues. How many weddings have you attended in an historical place, or in a hospital lobby or a gym? Maybe these will be your first and most memorable.

You will do me a great favor if you enjoyed this series and write a quick, honest review on Amazon or Goodreads. Just a few words mean a lot and encourage others to read it.

Thank you. If you would like to be connected to me for comments and conversation please sign up for my newsletter at www.bonnieengstrom.com and learn about my writing history. You can email me at bengstrom@hotmail.com. Please put SERIES <in caps) in the subject line. I would love to chat with you.

Special BONUS! The Candy Cane Series is ideal for group discussion, especially for book clubs. I have a special offer for book clubs for all of my books. If you are interested please email me at bengstrom@hotmail.com with CLUB <all caps) in the subject line.

Blessings,

Bonnie

CHAPTER ONE

"*I* am Cinderella, with no fairytale prince."

Natalie whispered to herself and tossed her ponytail over her shoulder before she started wiping down the free weights. Was this what her life had come to? Cleaning stuff? She was grateful for her small gym and the local residents who had joined it and used it almost daily. Some of them said they were uncomfortable in the huge workout areas of the chain gyms. They liked the more intimate surroundings, chatting with neighbors who they actually knew, not someone in another zip code.

But, she didn't have enough members to pay the bills.

It was six o'clock and she was about to close up for the day when Bill walked in.

"Am I too late?"

He was a new member she'd only seen once or twice. But, he caught her attention this evening, maybe with his question. He had a full head of graying hair, a firm face with few wrinkles and a wide smile. What seemed like a genuine one, not a come on. He was very attractive for an older man, and her heart skipped a beat.

She guessed him to be fifty plus. Maybe thirty years older than her. Did that matter? Melanie's stepfather Bruce was in his fifties. But, Melanie hated him. Still, Bill had always been a gentleman the few times she had seen him here. Being a black belt in karate, she felt comfortable with any male coming late to her gym.

She had been inspired to start the gym right after high school when her swim coach mentor Coach Douglas encouraged her. He had been supportive of all the Candy Cane swim team members' dreams for the future, but because she wanted to encourage physical health, he offered to make a small investment in Natalie's gym. He died before he could make it legal, nor support any of the other Candy Canes' endeavors. The other girls had pursued other dreams. Noelle had married Braydon who owned Love In Joy Floral Shop in Corona del Mar, and she was teaching English at Vista del Mar High School. Melanie was working at New Hope Preschool in aftercare, but would soon be promoted to teacher. Cindy had married her dream man on the beach in Costa Rica. She and Rob were missionaries planning to plant a church there and establish groups to support Multiple Sclerosis suffers. All important stuff. Connie was a fashion designer, and Doreen was one of her models. Candy had gotten married young, divorced and never pursued a career. Of all of them she was hands down the most beautiful.

What did Natalie have? She just ran a small gym. One that only attracted locals, mostly because they knew her. Her client base was small.

Dialing her phone, she called Candy, the encourager. After all, what were Candy Canes for? They were such a tight knit group, and they always prayed for each other.

~

"Me, too," Candy said when Natalie told her she was down in the dumps. "Do you think it's our age?"

Natalie laughed at that. "Maybe. But, hey, we ain't *that* old, girl."

"How about single?" Candy retorted.

"Candy," Natalie almost yelled. "We are only twenty-six. Not over the hill yet. In our prime. Still able to reproduce." Why had she said that? Was she desperate to have children, a family?

~

Bill came in the following morning. Early this time, real early. She said a simple "Hi" and went back to stacking free weights in their proper places. So frustrating that people used them and left them near machines or on the floor. Why hadn't she noticed them last night when she was wiping down? Maybe Bill coming in late distracted her.

This morning he waved and jumped on the treadmill, amping it up to high intensity. She could tell by the loud whirring sound. Last night he wore workout shorts and a short-sleeved tee. Today he wore long workout pants with a stripe down the legs and a tee shirt that hugged his biceps. Not bad ones for an older guy.

What was she thinking? Was she so desperate she was drawn to a man more than twice her age? He seemed a very nice man, a man who was almost handsome and was pleasant and courteous. But, what did she know about him? Maybe he was married, although no ring. But, many men of his era didn't wear rings. Wearing wedding bands was more of a millennial thing. Forget it, Natalie. Find another dream.

Several more clients came in. Kerstin Day, Noelle's mother, with a neighbor of hers. Natalie really should make more of an effort to memorize each client's name. When the gym started to fill up, she went to her office to do paper work. Bryce, her one personal trainer, clocked in and started to work with Kerstin. He was a blessing. All the clients loved him. If more clients wanted personal training at the same time, she would jump in. Unless she was giving a class.

She was paying her rent bill online and wondering how she would get through the next month. She looked at the sparse stack of checks on her desk. Some clients were late again. She felt uncomfortable reminding them, but business was business. She couldn't survive without their monthly payments. When she mentioned it the women would reach into their purses and pull out a check book. But, men almost always had to go to their cars and usually came back with cash. Then she had to write receipts. What was it with men and cash?

She flipped the lid closed on her laptop just as

she heard a tapping. Bill was smiling at her through the speckled glass insert of the door. He was so tall the top of his head was cut off from view. What could he want? He had already paid his bill as he did punctually on the first of every month. Maybe he wanted to report a damaged machine. She opened the door and smiled.

"May I come in? Want to chat with you about something, an idea."

She gestured to the straight back wood chair and returned to her own chair behind the desk. He perched on the edge of his mopping his forehead with a small white towel.

"What's up, Bill?" She hoped she didn't sound too confrontational, but she was due to start a Zumba class in ten minutes.

"Bad time? Sorry. I know you have a schedule to keep." he said. "This won't take long, but if it's something you are interested in discussing more, we could do so over coffee later."

Natalie nodded and squeezed her hands together on her desk.

"I've been thinking." He flung the towel around his neck.

She started to fidget. Would he ever get to the point? Then his face broke into that warm smile she liked so much, and the words from his mouth stunned her. Was he serious?

CHAPTER TWO

*H*e was offering her money!

At first she misunderstood, mainly because he had bungled the words. Nerves? Embarrassment? She felt sweat break out on her forehead, for him, not her. Poor man.

"I guess I messed that up." He wiped his face again with the towel and leaned forward placing his folded hands on the edge of the desk. This time he squinted. "I want to invest. In your gym."

He went on to say he knew how costly it was to rent space in Newport Beach, how he believed in young entrepreneurs and how he had a desire to support them. He also had a background in marketing, something Natalie knew little about and did very little of. She mumbled something like "Thank you. I will think it over. So nice of you."

Excusing herself, she shook his hand and practically pushed him out the door. Locking it behind her, she rushed to her class. One of the ladies, Claire, the take-over type, had already put the music on. For once, Natalie was glad for Claire's help. Sometimes the woman could be annoying, rushing to dim the lights and close the door before everyone was in the room. But, today she was grateful and thanked Claire who beamed at the compliment. She wished she could have Claire take over the class today. So much was spinning around in her head, so many scenarios. And questions. What were the real motives behind Bill's offer? If she accepted it, they would be working together closely, at least in the beginning. A contract would have to be signed; lawyers might have to be involved, and a lot of kinks would have to be worked out. Probably over a lot of coffee. Could she handle that emotionally?

~

"He what?" Candy shouted. Natalie pulled the phone away from her ear. *My word that girl has a strong voice.* Of course she knew that from Candy screaming encouragement when Nat was in the lane doing butterfly. But she figured she was yelling loud to be heard over the rush of water in Nat's ears. She reminded herself, that was over ten years ago.

"Yep. He really did offer to invest," Natalie said. "Did I tell you he's a looker?" She cleared her throat. "Bu … but, he's old."

"Like ancient old? Like eighty? An old codger?"

"More like fifty plus."

"Aw, oh. You sure this is the right thing to do?"

"I don't know. I'm confused, but I do need the money."

"Nat, I think this is something to share with the Candy Canes. Really."

Natalie knew Candy was right. She also knew Candy could keep a secret. She had certainly kept the one about Dev her ex-husband being an alcoholic for a long time. It wasn't until Cindy's wedding that she shared it; mainly because Rob shared his own struggle with alcoholism. But, that was a very different situation. If she did go ahead and accept Bill's offer, it wouldn't be secret for long. Even though she was sole owner of Nat's Gym, she wasn't LLC. She didn't know much, if anything, about forming a partnership. She needed advice.

"Before we spill the beans to others, I have an idea." She explained she would like advice from people who had been involved in the corporate world. She would ask Noelle's parents the Days and the Lovejoys, Rob and Braydon's parents. She guessed Nat's Gym wasn't too different from Love In Bloom Floral. Oh, why hadn't she become a teacher like Noelle?

~

"It sounds exciting, Natalie, but I would want to learn more. For instance, what is his background? Where is the investment money coming from? Lots of questions - need answers."

Natalie hung up the phone and agreed to a meeting with Logan Lovejoy and Darrell Day. The three would meet for coffee the following evening, but first she had an assignment.

She nabbed Bill the next morning just before he stepped on the treadmill. He was way ahead of her and pulled an envelope out of the machine's drink pocket. He suggested she take it to her office and read it. "Carefully," he said.

"I don't have any family here in California, and being the youngest of six girls, my dad is pretty old and retired. He's good at giving advice, but he never worked in the business world, just taught school." She waved the envelope like a fan, said "Thanks," and hoped Bill wouldn't be offended by her next statement. "I know two very savvy business people who can help me figure this out and make a decision. That okay with you?"

"Of course," he said. "I have nothing to hide. In fact, I'd love to meet them."

"Maybe. Soon."

She retreated to her office and slid a hefty wad of papers out of the envelope. One was a curriculum vitae several pages long; one was a legal document and, finally, several stapled together showed a business plan. Wow. Feeling overwhelmed, she shoved the papers back in the envelope. She would have Mr. Day and Mr. Lovejoy look them over this evening.

~

She spotted the two men at a corner table. Of course they were friends since their children had married each other; then Rob married a Candy Cane. Cindy was almost like a daughter to both families. All the Candy Canes were.

"I hope you don't mind that I brought Candy. I've always believed in another set of ears and eyes." The men smiled, nodded and stood up while the two women slid into the booth. Such gentlemen. So few nowadays. But, these men were from an era in which gentlemanliness was the expected norm. Actually, Bill was from the same era. The same one as her friends' fathers. Suddenly, he seemed old.

~

"So?" He tilted his head to look at her. He had knocked on her door the next morning right after the gym opened at six a.m. and settled himself in the wooden chair. "What did your mentors think?"

Natalie grinned. "They were actually quite impressed. You do your homework well, Mr. Lord. In fact both of them know you."

"Really? Who are they?"

"Logan Lovejoy and Darrell Day." She watched his face for a reaction and got it.

"Logie and Dar?" He slapped his knee and laughed. "How do you know them? Big time Mr. Investment Broker and Mr. Big Time Realtor." He laughed again. "I am anxious to hear the story."

Natalie explained a bit about the Candy Canes and how two of them had married a Lovejoy. How all the girls were like sisters and close to both families. What she still didn't understand was the connection between Bill and her friends' fathers. So, she asked.

At first his answer was evasive. Was he trying to protect someone's privacy? That made her uncomfortable. But, both Mr. Lovejoy and Mr. Day had said they were fine with her, and Bill, sharing the connection the three men had. She felt out of her league. She wished her own dad had been a big business man. But, until he retired, he had been first a social studies teacher for thirty years, then a school principal for almost ten. He was obviously smart, but not business savvy. Still, she was proud of him, loved him dearly and always sought his advice about personal things. Well, this was personal, wasn't it? She would call him tonight, maybe fax all the paperwork Bill had provided.

Finally, Bill spoke. "We did a massive real estate deal about ten years ago. Gave us all an edge financially. Well, more than an edge. Made us moderately rich."

Natalie tried to process that information. It was so foreign to her, but she had heard about deals like that. They were often in the paper, even on TV. All she could think about was how both the Days and the Lovejoys lived in big houses. But, neither of them were mansions by any stretch. Lots of people in Newport Beach lived in big houses. Probably burdened with enormous mortgages. She felt blessed to own a small one bedroom condo on the border of Newport and Costa Mesa, so her zip code was a Newport one. Not that it mattered. It was close to her gym, her favorite supermarket and not too far from church. Those were what mattered.

It was seven o'clock. She finished wiping down the equipment, picked up her laptop, turned off the overhead lights, closed the door and locked it. Stepping outside, she was looking forward to, actually craving, a bubble bath when a strong arm wrapped itself around her. She jumped.

"Sorry," Bill said. "Really sorry I frightened you. Meant to protect you."

"You scared the living daylights out of me." She hoped he heard the anger in her voice. What was he doing here? Now?

"Bad judgement on my part." He apologized again, this time with a softer tone.

"Please take your hands off me. I just want to go home." Had she said it strong enough?

"There's someone I want you to meet."

"Not tonight. Too tired." She pushed him away and clicked the key fob for her car door to unlock. Jumping inside and locking it, she revved the engine. Maybe overkill, but she didn't care. Was Bill Lord trustworthy? Had she been taken in by his proposal to invest in her gym, or had she been taken in by his handsome face? The way he filled out a tee shirt didn't hurt either. She was lonely, but was she desperate?

She thought about the way she'd pushed him off. Who was the person he wanted her to meet? This whole business about him possibly investing was getting complicated. Tomorrow she would call Login Lovejoy and Darrell Day again. She needed advice.

~

Bill would have kicked himself, if he could. Was he losing his touch? He really did care for Natalie, but he wasn't sure she understood. He pushed a button on his phone. "Hi, son. Are you up for a challenge?"

CHAPTER THREE

"Oh, my gosh! Oh, my gosh! Oh, my gosh!" Natalie couldn't stop repeating herself. "Candy," she said breathlessly, "you have to meet him. He's drop dead gorgeous!" Then she thought about the fact Candy had never met Bill, either.

"I'm game. When?" Natalie could visualize the wide-eyed grin on Candy's face. The girl had so much expression. Her eyes were probably rolling, curvy lips making indentations in her dimpled cheeks and eyebrows arched high. The Candy Canes had always dubbed Cindy The Strong One and Connie The Creative One, but Candy was The Expressive One, always making amusing faces. Noelle who loved clothes and dressed to kill was The Glam One. What had they called her, Natalie? Oh, The Organized One. Right now she just felt like The Flabbergasted One.

"I'll set it up. Or, maybe you should start working out at my gym. Then you could meet them both."

"I thought the dad was the one who joined your gym."

"Yes, and no." Natalie giggled. "Bill decided Bill Junior should join, too, since he's bringing him 'into the fold' as he calls it. 'A little father-son boding will be good for both of us,' he said. 'Boy needs to get a grip on life.'"

"What does that mean?" Candy asked. "Is young Bill a ne'er-do-well?"

"I dunno. He's in his late twenties, or maybe early thirties." She paused and thought. "Not sure what he does for a living, or if he has a job. But, for sure, he could be a male model. So gorgeous!"

"I'm dying to meet both of them. You still have a crush on the dad?"

"Uh, not sure. I do like maturity in a man, but Bill Senior has never revealed his marital status. Just come to the gym tomorrow morning about seven, my treat. I think they will both be there."

"Okay. I'll dig out my old workout duds" she agreed. "But, Nat, don't get emotionally involved until you know more, until you're sure." Natalie remembered that Candy's ex-husband, "Dev the Drunk," as she called him, was an older guy. She had been swept off her feet with wining and dining. After they'd been married a year, it was mostly wining.

~

Bill Senior showed up at six forty-five, again in his long pants and chest hugging tee. Just before seven Candy trotted in humming and swinging a flower printed gym bag. Natalie gave her a locker and led her over to meet Bill.

"Mr. Lord, this is my friend Candace, one of the Candy Canes I told you about." Bill slowed the treadmill, wiped his palm on his towel and gripped Candy's hand. His big smile showed he thought Candy was a looker. Especially, since he winked at her. What was that all about?

"Please, Natalie, and Candace, call me Bill. The Mister title makes me feel ancient." He looked over their heads as the door opened and grinned. "There's my boy now. Bill!" he shouted over the whir of the machines, "Come meet two lovely ladies."

Mr. Gorgeous, as Natalie had secretly dubbed him, reached them with long strides. His short light brown hair was slightly spiked, but the beard shadow on his angular jaws made him look like a print ad in a magazine. GQ? Natalie wondered what it would feel like to rub her cheek against it. *No, can't go there. His dad is the one I want.*

After all the introductions, Bill Junior jumped on the treadmill next to his dad. Candy approached the free weights lined up in front of the mirrored wall. Natalie noticed Candy's hands shook when she picked up the eight pound ones. Was it because she hadn't worked out for a while, or was it a reaction from meeting the two handsome men?

Natalie finished giving her Zumba class and was walking toward her office when she felt a muscular arm wrap around her shoulder and squeeze it. This time she didn't pull away. Both Candy and Bill Junior came toward them mopping their brows with towels.

"Coffee, ladies?"

Bill squeezed her shoulder again. What was he doing? First he winked at Candy, then started touching Natalie. She would never have guessed either gesture to come from him. Candy raised her brows on her animated face. She had obviously caught both, too.

"Sure!" Both girls spoke in unison.

"I'll leave Bryce in charge," Natalie said.

"Good," Bill said. "Since Nat and I, and possibly Billy, will be working together, we should get to know each other better."

Billy? Mmm. Wasn't that moniker a bit juvenile for Bill's son? Of course, he is the dad and probably called him that since he was born. Candy's mom called her grown son Billy. Must be a parent thing.

Natalie was trying to decide how to label both men privately. Big Bill and Little Bill? Old Bill and Young Bill? Didn't matter as long as she figured out how to tell them apart in her own mind. After they were seated at a corner table in IHOP, she asked, "So, gentlemen, how do each of you like to be called? It's confusing. Do either of you have a nickname? Especially you, Bill." She pointed to the younger man. She knew she was a stickler for detail, but really, it was puzzling.

"I guess we are both just Bill," Young Bill replied. "I know it must be confusing for you, especially just meeting us together. Mom had a certain inflection in her voice for each of us. Of course, she sometimes called me Junior."

Natalie and Candy both looked at him

quizzically. This time Natalie was sure her eyebrows were raised, too. She saw Candy's were.

"Mom's dead," he said. Older Bill nodded and made a ball wad of his napkin.

"So sorry," both girls said.

"It's okay. Dad and I have each other."

"Well, son, time you started looking to get hitched. I want grandchildren." Big Bill looked confused. "Sorry, inappropriate comment," he said when Young Bill glared at him.

Young/Little, or whatever she called him in her mind, spoke next. "Why don't you call me Junior?"

Both girls nodded and placed their coffee orders to the waitress.

~

"So, let me get this straight," Candy said when they got back to the gym. Natalie was glad the men hadn't insisted on escorting them, just walked them to her car. "Dad Bill is unhappy, at least not a hundred percent in favor that Junior is a male model. Wants him to be more traditional, be a business man."

They learned Junior had won an international modeling competition at nineteen and it sent him all over Europe. While in Italy, he'd been contracted with Ducati motorcycles. They even capitalized on his surname, Lord. In, what he worried, was an inappropriate way. Print ads and posters had phrases like, "The Lord revs it up on a Ducati!"

"Really upset Mom. She had a deep faith, and she thought using my last name that way was both deceptive and dishonoring to Christ. But," he continued, "I hadn't chosen it. I guess I could have insisted the company not use my name at all. I tried, but the big wigs reminded me of the contract I'd signed. Guess that was a big reason they signed me." He had lowered his head over his coffee. "It was a five year contract, would have meant copious legal tape to get out of it, especially in another country. Now, I pose only for American cycles. Still," he had looked at his dad, "Dad doesn't see it as a real job." He paused. "I asked forgiveness, and I believe God told me I had been a naive kid with hopes too high."

~

The girls were having another cup of coffee, this time with flavored creamer, at Candy's house where she lived with her mom. "I don't think what he did was so bad," Candy said. "He was young, a kid, and excited about what a future in modeling could offer." She looked at Natalie. "What?"

Nat wasn't sure. She wanted to believe Junior (was that really a name?), but she had reservations. She was disappointed that Bill Senior wasn't more supportive of his son. After all, Junior had gotten his good looks from his parents, and initially, according to Junior, they had been very supportive of his chosen career.

Candy's mom wandered into the kitchen to make a cup of tea. "What are you girls talking about?" So, they told her.

~

Vivian Ashford asked point blank. "So who's in love with who?"

Both girls laughed. "No one is in love with anyone. Yet."

"Mmm. I couldn't help overhearing you talking about a handsome duo." She filled a cup with water and put it in the microwave. Pushing a button, she said, "Which one is Bill?"

The girls laughed again. "Both," Natalie said. Mrs. Ashford looked confused.

"How can that be? Unless … unless it's just a coincidence, or," she paused and raised an eyebrow, "they are father and son."

This time the girls nodded while laughing.

"So," she asked, "ages?"

They explained the whole situation to her while she dipped a tea bag in her mug. Adding sugar, she plunked it on the table, pulled out a chair and looked at both of them with concern. "You," she said pointing at Candy, "steer clear of the older one. You have been there, done that. And, hopefully learned your lesson."

Looking at Natalie, she repeated the finger pointing. "You have also hopefully learned a lesson from Candy. May December marriages don't work out. Not much, anyway," she asserted. "However, in most cases it's the man who gets the bad end of the situation."

Natalie knew the Ashfords had been through a lot of pain and agony with Candy's choice of a husband and her divorce. Now, because of it and the legal fees it had imposed, Candy couldn't afford to live on her own. In fact, she still didn't have a job after two years of searching. But, just because Bill Senior was older, maybe close to Candy's parents' ages, didn't mean he would be a repeat of misery for her. Besides, Natalie was attracted to him, not necessarily Candy. Or, was she wrong?

When Candy's mom left to do laundry, the girls stared at each other. Natalie made a little circle on the table of a small puddle of coffee. "That was interesting," she said. "You okay with it?"

Candy shrugged. Natalie guessed Mrs. Ashford was right. Candy should steer clear of Bill Senior. She didn't see him as a cradle robber, but sometimes older men who had lost a wife were really taken by a young, pretty woman. And, Candy was definitely that.

"You saw him first." Candy bumped Natalie's arm playfully with her fist. "Still, I think he's too old for either of us. Maybe one of us will have to settle for Junior." She giggled. "Or, maybe Junior has a girlfriend."

"Hope not. But, it would serve us both right for dreaming." Natalie kept playing with the coffee puddle. "He really is drop dead gorgeous, but not my type." She looked at the wet, brown tip of her finger.

"Don't give me the 'I like the mature type.' The only semi-serious boyfriend you had was that goofy guy who graduated high school three years ahead of us. He wasn't even close to mature."

"Yeh. He was a loser."

"So glad you saw that then. But, you were pretty broken up when he ditched you for not wanting to romp in the backseat of his funky car."

"I was young. Loved the attention. He lettered in basketball." She kept rubbing her finger in the coffee.

"Thank the Lord you were a strong Christian

girl. I wish some of your faith had rubbed off on me."

"What you could have used with Devin was discernment. You had faith – too much faith in love."

"Guess we'd better get going and face the music." Candy pushed her chair back and bumped Natalie on the arm.

"Guess so." She didn't sound enthused, even to herself. Maybe the relationship with Bill Lord Senior, professional or personal, wasn't such a good idea. Especially, personal. But, the two seemed destined to blend.

CHAPTER FOUR

*T*he girls had agreed the men could pick them up for an early dinner date. They figured it would save them gas and what was the harm in it? They'd even decided one would sit in front with whomever was driving, and after dinner they would switch. They would be very assertive about it. They waited outside Nat's Gym, both in pants as the Bills had requested. They had no idea why. Maybe the men were going to take them to the Fun Zone on Balboa to ride the bumper cars, or one of those ferry rides past the movie stars old houses. They stood on the curb pulling their sweaters around them in the chilly evening air. They expected a car to round the corner, until …

The roar was so loud they both held hands over their ears. Motorcycles!

"No, no, no," Natalie exclaimed. "I will not ride one of those."

"Come on, Nat. Be a sport. I even brought you

a helmet, and Billy brought one for Candy, too." He dug into what she assumed was the equivalent of a car trunk for a Harley and pulled out a silver helmet. Holding it out to her, he said, "It's really very safe. We aren't going that far. Try it on."

"I don't wear headgear that others have worn. When I was ten I had lice from a riding helmet I borrowed. Scared the pants off me. Oops. Bad analogy." She shook her head. "We will take my car."

"Scaredy cat!"

Natalie couldn't believe Candy goaded her. "You can ride one of these contraptions. I'll follow in my car. Where are we going, anyway?"

Candy popped on a shiny white helmet and jumped on the back of Junior's cycle. Wrapping her arms around his torso, she looked back at Natalie. "It's really fun, Nat, and safe."

Natalie still shook her head. What was Candy doing? Then she remembered how wild the girl was in high school. Maybe that's why she was so attracted to Devin the Drunk. He appealed to her wild streak.

Well, she was the practical, organized one of the Candy Canes. They always came to her for advice from reorganizing closets to how to label stuff. Her mom had told her it was a gift and God was using her. Still, she never felt creative like Connie who designed beautiful clothes, or free spirit hang loose like Candy was now. Maybe she should bend a little, especially if she was interested in one of the Bills. Which she wasn't, of course.

She raised her hand. "Wait up. I will try." She

looked Bill Senior square in the face, partially hidden by his big helmet. "You promise I'll be safe?" He nodded and grinned. "Who wore the helmet?" The threat of disease, and nits, frightened her.

"Only my wife. That okay?"

She placed the bulky thing on her head, and he helped her adjust it. Clinging to him with arms wrapped around, she closed her eyes and prayed. She silently repeated Psalm 23 and clung harder. She felt her fingernails digging into his leather jacket. At least the helmet had a sort of face mask. "So bugs won't bug you," Bill teased her.

~

When the cycle stopped vibrating, and she did, too, she cautiously put a toe of her shoe on the ground and started to slide off. Her legs were so short she almost fell sideways. Junior caught her just as she listed. His enticing scent smelled so good she almost lingered in his strong arms.

Her legs felt like stretched out rubber bands with no elasticity left. What would her mother have said? "Stretched to the limit." What, she wondered, was her limit?

She wobbled to the door of the restaurant, clinging to Bill's arm on unsteady feet. Gripping his arm tighter, she recognized where they were. The Cannery!

"This is the restaurant we Candy Canes come to once every year before Christmas for our annual get-together. I know it well. Even know what I will order."

"What will you order?"

"Oysters."

~

Bill couldn't believe how many oysters on the half shell Nat had sucked down. He even took a photo. Maybe he would send it to her.

He was both stunned and delighted Natalie was enjoying herself. And, that she had accepted the ride on his bike, even though reluctantly. When he had first approached her about investing in her gym, he was sincere. He still hoped to be, but looking at her cute button nose as she slurped in each oyster with rosy lips gave him shivers down his legs and second thoughts in his brain. Maybe his heart. Maybe other places.

He made every effort to not look below her face. That was hard. He knew she had a toned body. He had seen it. Peripheral vision? Probably, but it was now just starting to compute.

It had been three years since Marsha had died. Breast cancer was such a horrible disease. The first year after her death he had devoted to supporting cancer research, giving a lot of money and even showing up at rallies. He'd never had the nerve, or maybe the stamina, to do the walk. Now, after two years of physically working out, he knew he could, but wasn't sure he wanted to. Time and healing had passed. Maybe his heart wasn't in it anymore.

Bill made another joke about Natalie's overabundance of oysters and paid the server. When the young man removed their plates his eyes got huge. Bill shook his head and quietly said, "The lady really enjoyed them. Didn't you, Nat?" She nodded, grinned and thanked him for the indulgence.

Offering his arm, she slipped her hand in the crook of his elbow. The sun was glinting on the water and casting shadows from nearby anchored boats. Bill Junior and Candy stumbled behind them trying not to slip on the ramp that led from the restaurant.

"Gosh, Dad," young Bill said, "nothing has changed here since I was a kid."

Bill remembered this had been a fun restaurant to bring him to because of the cans on the ceiling that slowly moved above them while they were eating.

Both Bills led the girls to the cycles. Both girls hesitated. Bill couldn't understand why since they'd had such a fun ride. He asked Natalie.

"I guess I'm still a little shaky. First time," she confessed. "I'd rather ride horses."

"Really? Why? Horses scare me."

"They don't vibrate," she said. "And you can bond with them. Lovely creatures."

She had looked him square in the face. "Why don't you go riding with me? Sunday afternoon. After church, of course."

Now he was stuck. He was terrified of horses after the one time he'd gone trail riding with Marsha, at her insistence. Apparently, the big mare didn't like him. He still remembered eating dirt and Marsha laughing. "She sensed your fear, Bill. Don't let her win. Dust off, stroke her nose, give her one of those treats in your pocket, talk gently to her, and hop back on." Marsha was a horse woman; it was her first love. After him.

Fear overtook him again. He was a grown man in his fifties he reminded himself.

"I don't know. Had a bad experience once. Got thrown."

"Did you get hurt? Badly."

"Not really. Just scared."

"Like I was riding the cycle?"

"But," he said with conviction, "I can control the cycle."

She clapped her hands together and laughed so loud he almost walked away. What was it with this woman? Was she a vixen in disguise? Until this evening he thought she was sweet and kind and sensitive. And, what about the church thing? Would he have to attend, too? Before the horrifying, bloodcurdling task of riding.

CHAPTER FIVE

"Billy called." Candy sensed the hesitation in Nat on the other end of the phone.

"Which one?" Nat asked.

"Bro." Candy reluctantly explained. "He saw me, us, on the cycles the other night. Wanted to know what I was doing acting like a teenager with a low life. He has always been judgmental."

"What did you say?"

"Ow! Striker!"

"What was that about?"

"I walk when I talk on the phone, as you probably know, and I tripped on one of the stupid dog's toys."

"And, you don't look where you are going!" Nat chuckled.

"There are too many Bills and Billys in my life."

"We need to sort them out."

"But, how?"

"Maybe a code? Like one, two, bro?"

"Did you know Dev's middle name was also William?"

"This is ridiculous, makes it even more complicated," Natalie replied. "Have you heard from either of the two motorcycle Bills? It's been at least two days. Should I be worried? I mean about Big Bill, aka Old Bill, investing? Or, do you think he's backed out?"

"Have either been to the gym lately?"

"Not when I've been there. But, I do take breaks for coffee and lunch. Especially after doing a class. Still, everyone has to sign in, and I haven't seen either name."

"I think you should call him. Or, one of them."

"That seems forward."

"No, Nat, not if he was, still is, sincere about a deal for your gym." Candy gripped the phone harder. "Natalie, you have to be realistic. You need the money, you need the support. Don't pass up this opportunity." Candy was so frustrated with Natalie she almost pressed the red button on the phone. Finally, she shouted, "Get real, girl. Please!" Then, she put down the receiver.

~

Candy stared at her email inbox. Pushed the inbox line again to be sure. Yes, it was from Cindy pleading. From Costa Rica. She felt guilty she hadn't written to Cindy and Rob lately. They needed support, if only moral. They had assumed a huge responsibility, left everything behind and started a new life – on faith. She noticed Cindy had sent the email to several others in Cc – carbon copy.

Guess she was pretty desperate.

> Dear Friends,
>
> This is a hard post to write, but we need support. Rob has had several 'incidents' with his MS and some days can hardly walk. He takes his medication daily, does the prescribed exercises and even runs a small support group. Three other people in the housing complex have MS, so it's an intimate group. Rob also attends two AA meetings every week, most of them conducted by Brian who is the manager of the bungalow rentals. Brian has been sober for over ten years, so he is a great mentor for Rob. Since Rob can still swim in the community pool, his legs seem to work well in water, Brian thinks he should surf. Frankly, that frightens me. Still, Brian would be with him, and he is a strong swimmer and used to surf all the time in Newport.
>
> As for me. I have not had the interest and success I hoped for to start a church. Some of the people I approach are very kind, but others look at me as if I am an alien with five heads. I wonder sometimes why God led us here. I cling to Jeramiah 29:11 as my hope. It has always been my favorite Bible verse. But, right now I feel so empty.
>
> I am not asking for financial support, although since we are depleting our savings, that would be very helpful. But, I trust God and you. He will provide. I just need to have each of you tell me you are praying for us, and that you believe in us and love us.
>
> Your friend in Christ,
> Cindy

Candy laid her head down on the computer

keyboard and cried. Her friend needed her, and she didn't know how to help. Had Natalie gotten the same message? She called her and asked.

~

"Yes," Natalie said, "sadly I did." Candy wiped her eyes again. "What can we do?" Nat asked.

"I know I'm not good at this organizational stuff like you," Candy offered, "but could we organize a prayer vigil for them? Like on a weekly or even daily basis?"

"Don't people who do that look a little desperate?"

"Nat! What are you saying? It doesn't have to be public. And, yes," she yelled, "it is desperate."

"We could certainly send a small amount to them, even give our tithe to them instead of church. But, will that help?"

"Check out Malachi 3:10, Nat. Yes, it will not only help, but it will fill the needs to overflowing." Candy almost slammed down the phone, she was so frustrated. Did Natalie not have the same concerns she did for Cindy and Rob?

Finally, Natalie asked, "Do you think a vigil would do any good?"

~

They announced a vigil prayer time for Cindy and Rob to take place every Friday morning at Nat's Gym from six to six-fifteen. Not a long time, but enough to start. Notice went out to all clients. Nat and Candy wondered who would respond.

Would some feel intimidated? Would some feel Nat's Gym was only for believers? Would some cancel their gym memberships? This coming Friday would tell the tale. It was a big risk for Natalie.

~

Bill opened his email inbox and scratched his head. What? A Candy Cane prayer vigil? Starting tomorrow? He knew the girls were Christians, but wouldn't this stamp a big cross on Natalie's business? He read the email again.

Dear Members,

Many of you know I am a member of a special group of women called the Candy Canes. We have been close friends for over ten years, and we support each other in many ways. One of us, Cindy, and her husband Rob Lovejoy are serving as missionaries in Costa Rica with plans to plant a church, and for Rob who has multiple sclerosis to form support groups for others with MS.

The other day all the rest of us got a sad email from Cindy. Although Rob's first support group is small, only three others besides him, it is steady and has been very helpful to those involved. However, Cindy said Rob has had several MS flare-ups causing him to have difficulty walking sometimes. Yet, he remains upbeat and dedicated. The man is a trooper.

Unfortunately, they have had very little success interesting people in starting a new church. Cindy says people are either kind or look at her like she has five heads.

She is not asking for financial help. She is asking for prayer. We want to give it to them.

She and Rob have some financial support from their home church in Irvine, CA. As dedicated missionaries, Mariners Church pays their rent and a small stipend for living expenses. Cindy, whom all the

Candy Canes have always designated Leader of the Group (she swam freestyle, starting off every swim meet and taking the lead for the rest of us), is very discouraged. This is so unlike her.

Two of us, Natalie who owns Nat's Gym and Candace, have decided to give her what she asks for – prayer.

We will be holding a prayer vigil for Cindy and Rob every Friday morning in Nat's Gym from 6-6:15 a.m. This is not obligatory. We ask that only believers attend. No names will be taken. It will be as anonymous as possible. No need to reply. Just show up.

Thanks for your attention. We hope we haven't put anyone in an uncomfortable situation.

Natalie and Candace

PS ~ Please feel free to bring friends.

~

Bill scratched his head again, then called his son. "What do you make of this, Billy?"

"I think it's great, Dad. Those girls are go-getters, and they have a lot of faith and bravery."

"But, won't this put her gym on the line? Especially, the part about my investing in it?"

"Maybe, Dad, you should call Natalie's mentors, the Lovejoy and Day men." He paused, and Bill could hear the frustration in his son's voice. "Since they are both very successful and both Christians, I think they could give you a lot of insight. And comfort," he added. "You did some kind of deal with them before, didn't you? So, you know them, and they should both be open to your concerns."

Bill pondered his son's advice and scratched

his head again. What was wrong with him, with his faith? He would show up tomorrow for the first prayer vigil, keep his head low and arrive from his car parked two blocks away. No noisy motorcycle.

~

Candy and Natalie walked into the gym at five-thirty. Both were anxious. Would this be a good thing, this prayer meeting? They stood together holding hands and prayed for God's will. When Natalie opened the doors to the gym at five-fifty-five, they saw a small crowd outside.

Twenty or so people rushed to the door. Bill Senior was first in line.

Natalie hugged him, as she did to all the people coming to pray for Cindy and Rob. When he released her she felt funny sensations in her tummy. Maybe it was just because he was the first to appear.

She had asked Candy to take over. She was so much more confident than Nat.

Natalie gestured for everyone to crowd into the small seating area in the gym where some older members often waited for their rides after a workout. Although most had to stand today, everyone had a beaming face. She was amazed.

"Thank you all for coming," Candy said. "I know this is unprecedented, very unusual. And that," she continued, "is what makes it so special.

"Let me tell you a little about the Candy Canes, so you will understand why we are here."

Everyone clapped.

She briefly explained about the high school swim team and how they had gotten together in the beginning, when Coach Douglas had singled each of them out. How they had won four state championships, and especially how their faith had brought them all together for so many years.

"We are sisters," she said. "We will always support each other, always be there for each other. And, that," she concluded, "is why we are here today. To support a sister.

"So, if you are here to support our sister Cindy, let us pray."

~

Bill had passed around a basket. Candy and Nat were appalled, but it was his thing, not theirs. They didn't want to stop it because it really could help Cindy and Rob. But, it was not what they had intended, so it was somewhat embarrassing. At least Bill made it clear it was his idea, not theirs.

Nat and Candy were blessed when many of the people who attended prayed out loud. Bill had also had the foresight to record the prayers on his cell phone. Candy would send them to Cindy later.

Just before the prayer vigil broke up with many Amens, Claire, the often difficult member of Nat's Zumba class, spoke up loudly.

"This," she announced, "is a golden opportunity to bless. May we pray daily for this couple, and I would like to make a suggestion for them."

Everyone either gasped or looked to her skeptically. Some turned away and left. What would she suggest?

Claire suddenly blossomed. Who was this take over woman, Nat wondered? Until she heard her.

"I am a mother. I have never publicly professed my faith before, but I am now. Because of Rob Lovejoy, my son Nick is now sober."

A few women grasped their hands together and held them against their hearts. Heads nodded and throats cleared.

"I would like to set up a GoFundMe account for Rob and Cindy. As Candy said, it is not about money. But, realistically, money wouldn't hurt, and it can help." Claire looked around and Natalie and Candy saw several nodding heads. She passed out a list for people to sign up on with their email addresses. She asked they pass on the information to others. Then, she said, "Thank you Natalie and Candy for having this special meeting for your sister." Claire walked to her car, opened the door and slid inside with a wave.

Natalie and Candy hugged with tears in their eyes. Both Bills enveloped them with strong arms.

"I think this calls for a very special motorcycle ride," Bill Senior said. Bill Junior nodded.

CHAPTER SIX

"What crazy scheme have you gotten yourself involved in now?"

Candy's brother, Billy, was shouting at her. She put her phone down on the sofa next to her. She could still hear him, even though she hadn't pushed the speaker button. She had been trying to rest and make sense of the morning and, especially, the afternoon. The motorcycle ride had set her on edge. What had happened there? Somehow, she had ended up sitting behind Big Bill, as she mentally dubbed him, and not Little Bill where she had hoped to be. She had wrapped her arms around his torso and clung digging fingers into a soft leather jacket. Her nose ended up at the base of his neck, a neck that smelled so good. Something happened to her body then. It quivered, and her knees got weak and rubbery. But, her arms that clung to his body got stronger, and her own body seemed to melt into his back. She hadn't wanted to let go.

"Sis, are you there? Will you talk to me?" Billy's voice boomed over the cell phone. "Please explain what you are doing."

Candy sighed and reluctantly picked up the phone. "What do you think I'm doing? What do you care? And, if you don't stop shouting at me, I'm going to hang up."

"Sorry. I worry about you, and I worry about Nat." He paused to make a tch sound clacking his tongue against the roof of his mouth. "Her gym is going to be labelled. You know what I mean." Candy heard disgust in his voice.

"So? Suddenly you care about Nat's gym?" She heard the disgust in her own voice. "What has come over you, Billy?" Then it hit her. Billy has a thing for Nat. Yep, that was it. Had to be.

He did take her to his senior prom, but that was over eight years ago. When they were kids. Had they been secretly dating since then, or even lately? Surely, Nat would have told her. There weren't many secrets between Candy Canes. Except the one she had kept about Dev the Drunk, her ex-husband. Now, since Cindy and Rob's wedding, everyone knew because she had shared. She decided to change the subject.

"So, big bro, how's the used car business?" She always got a kick out of calling Billy a used car salesman. Actually, he was. He made tons of money reselling exotic cars like Lamborghinis, Lotuses and vintage Porches. She knew how to push his buttons, knew he couldn't resist telling her about his latest coup.

"Sold a 1960 Porche Speedster in perfect

condition yesterday. Not a scratch on it; convertible, silver. Guy said he'd had one in college, brought back his youth. Nice guy with silver hair. Paid cash." She could hear the thrill in his voice, the pride. She imagined he closed shop for about a half hour after the sale and ran right to the bank. She knew Billy didn't like to keep large sums in his office. Too risky on the Coast Highway.

"Good for you. Congrats." She hoped he had been distracted from his reason for calling. She hoped wrong.

"Now," he said. "Back to your crazy antics. You and Nat."

"They're not crazy, Billy. They're sincere. We are praying for support for Cindy and Rob who have run into a hiccup, so to speak."

"Rob's health giving them problems?" He did sound concerned. They had been old friends who drifted away from each other when Rob went into real estate and Billy into the car business. An investment group had financed Billy somewhat anonymously. They called themselves The Memory Men, but their names were top-secret. Somehow they kept their identities hush-hush, even from Billy. A representative of the bank acted as the go-between. Candy wasn't sure if that person actually knew whom he was representing – just did the paperwork. She pulled her thoughts back to Billy's question.

"Cindy said he's had a few incidents with his legs; trouble walking. He is fine swimming, though, which is recommended to MS patients. Might try surfing again. But, that scares her."

"Aw, shoot! Poor guy." She could hear the anger in his voice. Years ago he and Rob had surfed together. It was their one bond. But, life and success had gotten in the way and led them down different paths. Suddenly, she had an idea.

"Do you miss surfing?" She heard a sigh on the other end.

"Yeh. I still go out occasionally, like a few times a year. I went out with Stevens about a month ago. But, he's more into boarding – trying to teach his son." Another pause, then a sucked in breath. "Yeh. I miss it, a lot. Just no time anymore."

That was her cue, and she said a quick prayer when she took it. "You could go with Rob."

"What do you mean? He's thousands of miles away in a third world country."

"Billy, you can afford to visit." She knew he could, and she knew it would be good for him. Not just Rob. "You could use a break, and it would be great for both of you."

"You're kidding, right?"

"Not at all. You would love it there, and you didn't get to go to the wedding because you were so tied up with some negotiation for some silly car."

"It was a 2005 Bugatti Veyron! A 'silly car' worth millions."

"Oops. I stand corrected." Candy was glad he couldn't see her roll her eyes. Yikes! For sure he could afford to go to Costa Rica. "Billy," she persisted, "take a risk. Take a leap of faith. Go – for yourself, and for your friend."

She could almost hear the wheels spinning in his head. Grasping the phone so tightly her hand ached she appealed to the Holy Spirit.

~

"Oh, my gosh! Oh, my gosh!" Cindy's voice came over the two thousand miles clearly. They had finally figured out how to get a phone to call the U.S. One of the pastors from Mariners Church had brought them one with a California area code when he was passing through on his way to a mission in Guatemala. They had borrowed Brian's car and drove to Juan Santamaría International Airport in San Jose where the pastor was changing planes. Cindy said she felt like she was holding precious gold when he handed her the phone. He had written instructions about how to connect it to their computer. Candy heard the excitement in her voice, and her eyes filled with tears of joy.

"Yes," Candy said, "he really is coming."

"Next week? I don't think I can wait that long." Cindy giggled.

After they caught up, and Cindy shared that Rob's flare-ups had subsided, they prayed. It was a prayer of praise. Finally, Candy told her friend about the prayer vigils.

"You're doing that for us?" Candy nodded through her tears, then realized Cindy couldn't see her.

"You betcha. That's what Candy Canes do for each other."

"Oh, Candy, I am so grateful." Candy could hear sniffles on the other end. "How many people did you say showed up? Did Noelle, Doreen, Connie and Melanie come?"

"Noelle and Braydon, her mom, his mom, and

yes the other Candy Canes. Plus, the dads. Some people from Nat's gym; a woman named Claire who is going to start a GoFundMe for you and Rob, Kerstin Day's neighbor, a few I don't know and the Bills. About twenty-one in all. I counted."

"W – who are the Bills? Was Billy your brother one of them?"

"No, he didn't attend, but promised he would pray at his dealership. Maybe," she said a bit sarcastically, "he's coming to visit out of guilt." She knew she didn't mean it, but it had been pretty easy to sway him.

"Work be …!" he'd blurted out. "I do need a vacation. Where did you say I could stay?"

"You didn't answer my question. Or, was it too loaded?" Cindy asked, her voice full of curiosity.

"Uh. Later. I will email you, okay?"

"Okay. Speaking of emailing, do you think Billy would be willing to bring an extra suitcase?"

"I guess. Guys never pack a lot. Why?"

"It's the only way we can get certain things – to have someone travelling here bring them. If you shipped them they would never arrive. Remember how we brought the flowers for my wedding?"

"Do I! If we hadn't packed them in our luggage, they would have been love bunches for the customs men's women." She chuckled remembering the delicate flowers wrapped in Cellophane with plastic water holders on each stem. "Send me a list, but make it specific so Nat and Billy and I won't have to guess."

"Thank you. I will, and please tell Billy how special it will be to see him. I think Rob is ready to try to surf again. Brian surfs every day. So, with him and Billy looking out for Rob, I will be more comfortable."

Candy hung up, then remembered Claire's other idea. Well, she would email it to Cindy. It just might work.

CHAPTER SEVEN

Natalie was cleaning again. Wiping machines and mirrors. On a Saturday. She would have to talk with the crew she'd hired to clean every night. It was morning, five-forty-five, and there was lint on the floor and handprints on the mirrors. Not to mention the restrooms. Ugh. She hated confrontation, but she couldn't afford to pay for lackadaisical effort. Maybe if Bill invested she could hire a better cleaning crew for more money.

Bill bopped in at six on the dot while she was still wiping. He grabbed the dirty rag out of her hand. The scowl on his face told it all. "Doesn't your cleaning crew do this? Do you have one?"

She explained the budget wouldn't allow for a better one, and that she planned to come in at ten this evening and read them the riot act. He "harrumphed." She laughed. That made her feel better. Didn't solve the problem, but put a little pleasure in the day ahead.

"I will meet you here at nine-fifty-five. I will handle it."

Wow! Maybe he really was a fairytale prince. Her cellphone rang. Candy. She turned away from Bill to chat.

"Got an idea after I hung up with Cindy last night. Actually," she said, "that Claire woman gave it to me."

She reminded Natalie about Cindy's hopes for church planting, and how they had met with a wall. But, not an impenetrable one, she believed. "God knocks down walls," she said with enthusiasm. "Says so in Lamentations. Actually, they 'wasted away.' He also says in Joshua, 'I will give you every place where you set your foot.' I think verse 3 in chapter one. That's a good one for each of us. For you, Nat, about your gym, and for Melanie about the preschool." She cleared her throat. "I think that's my new favorite verse."

"You have to send that to her," Nat said. "Immediately. To give her encouragement and hope. I know she is a strong believer. But, I do remember she is not great at remembering Scripture. Maybe," she continued, "you should pack a few special books in that suitcase Billy will take. Like The Circle Maker. She could walk around the housing complex every day and pray like Mark Batterson did in D.C."

"Great idea. Goes right along with mine. I was thinking if she and Rob started a couples' Bible study, a low-keyed one, it might be a beginning for starting a church."

"Perfect. Let's go to Family Christian

tomorrow and find just the right ones."

~

Kris, the manager who often prayed with Candy among the stacks, led the girls to the Bible study section.

"But, we need about twenty books, not too expensive, okay cheap, that couples can read together."

"They need to be small and lightweight, too."

Kris led them to the Couples' section of the Clearance items. Natalie picked up one, leafed through it, and put it back. "Too detailed. Need something for barely believers. Not too heavy. More focused on life today, how to cope."

Candy explained what they were trying to do, and why. She told Kris about Cindy and Rob's mission. She almost saw a lightbulb shine above Kris' head.

She took them to the section that featured Bible studies. "They aren't on sale, but they are pretty inexpensive. I think these two might work." she pointed to two slim books on the shelf.

She first picked up a copy of Courageous Living Bible Study by Catt, Kendrick & Kendrick. Kris explained, "It has an introduction, a guideline for small groups and only four studies, each just ten pages. It's from the creators of Fireproof and also has a movie if you want it."

Nat nodded. "Any others?" Candy asked.

"I like this one a lot." Kris handed each of the women a book. "I think the title says it all." She grinned broadly, and when the women grinned back, she looked pleased. "It does have six studies, but I think it would appeal to moralistic people, or as you call them 'barely believers.'"

Natalie read the title aloud. "Character – Who You Are When No One's Looking. Perfect! I love it."

"And," Candy said, "it's by Bill Hybels who is Sr. Pastor of Willow Creek Community Church which is pretty famous, like Saddleback and Mariners."

"How many copies do you have, Kris? They have to be taken in Candy's brother's suitcase."

"I know. I've heard it's a wasted effort to mail anything to Costa Rica." Kris raised her eyebrows and formed a tight line with her lips. "So sad. Of course, we could pray over them and trust that God will see they get put in the right hands."

Natalie laughed. "We will pray over them anyway. We both do trust God, but you know the old saying our grandmas used. 'God helps those who help themselves.'"

"Yep. My grandma used to say that as a sort of threat to get me to do my homework." Kris chuckled.

The women counted the books. There were only five of the first one. Kris said she would call some of the other Family Christian stores for more copies. There were eight of the Character book, so the women took them all and waited while Kris called other stores for the Courageous Living book.

"The store near where I live has three copies and several study guides. I can pick them up on my way home this evening and have them here for you tomorrow. Would that work?"

Natalie pulled out a credit card and passed it to Kris at the cash register. "Oh, forgot to mention," Kris said, "if you buy one at full price, there will be a coupon at the bottom of your receipt for twenty percent off the entire next purchase you make." She peered closely at a notice next to the register. "Says it starts tomorrow. So, why don't I hold all the rest for you until then?"

Candy and Natalie linked arms and almost skipped to Nat's car like toddlers. "We are so blessed," Nat said.

"And," Candy responded, "we are blessing Cindy."

CHAPTER EIGHT

*C*andy and Natalie were huddled in front of Nat's computer in her little office reading Cindy's list.

"Chips?"

"Chips!"

"Chips?" The loud voice boomed through the partially opened door. Bill Senior stepped in with a quizzical expression on his face. "Poker chips? You girls ordering poker chips online?"

Both women got hysterical. Candy wiped her eyes and Natalie grabbed a tissue to blow her nose. When they finally stopped laughing, partly at Bill's question and partly, as Nat said later, the expression on his face, they shouted in unison, "NO!"

"C – corn chips," Nat blubbered. She was still trying to control her laughter. "A special brand. For Cindy in Costa Rica. Candy's brother is going there and taking stuff for her and Rob."

"We were reading her shopping list." Candy gestured to the computer. "In her email."

Bill still looked puzzled. "Can't she buy corn chips there? It is a Latino country, isn't it? Surely they sell corn chips."

"Yes, but she says they are thick and tough. She found a special brand here in the states that are thin and crispy, and low cal. Nachos are her specialty, even her recipe for them is published in a book." Nat blew her nose again. It was probably turning crimson. How embarrassing.

Candy explained. "It's a brand made by some famous food company. It's called $2 Only."

Bill cocked his head and winked. "Sure it is. Come on."

"Really, Bill. I've seen them on the shelves." Natalie huffed. "You don't believe us?"

"Uh, yeh, guess so." He changed the subject. "Place looks sparkling this morning." He was grinning from ear to ear.

"Oh, it does. Thank you so much for last night. You really did the trick." Nat beamed.

Candy looked askance with eyebrows raised.

"No, no." Nat explained how Bill had firmly let the cleaning crew know they needed to do better, be more thorough. "He didn't even have to yell, just gave them the look."

"What was that look?" Candy couldn't resist teasing. She looked Bill directly in the face, and he complied with a fierce scowl.

The girls burst into laughter again. They agreed later he did have an elastic face.

They asked Bill to excuse them so they could continue reading Cindy's list. He left for the gym shutting the door behind him. Both girls sighed loudly. "That was fun, but we'd better get back to work. I have a class in twenty minutes, and if I don't hustle, Claire will take over for me." Nat giggled. "Although not a bad idea. Claire would keep everyone in line."

~

Nat and Candy printed out two copies of the list, one for each. They each starred the items they would buy, agreeing to remove things from packages that would take up too much room. Except, of course, the chips. They had learned from the trip to Cindy and Rob's wedding that most food items could be brought into Costa Rica as long as they were labeled Made in the U.S.A. Nothing from China, or even European countries they thought.

They had also heard that some people travelling from the states were able to take in steaks as long as they had the U.S.A. label. Cindy thought it would be a special treat to send them some filet mignons from Costco, a flank steak and a small pork roast.

"But, that's too heavy," Nat protested. "Billy will have to pay extra duty."

"He can afford it," Candy replied with a twinkle in her eyes.

"He can? Why am I not dating him?"

That comment gave the duo another laugh. Natalie went to conduct her Zumba class, and Candy left to wait for her mom to pick her up. She still couldn't afford a car, but she knew God would provide when the time was right.

~

Candy shuffled on the sidewalk. Hopefully, Mom would come soon. Her birthday was in two weeks. Maybe God would send her a car for a present. "Not too likely," she mumbled to herself. Still, she would be happy if it was a clunker, just something to get from point A to point B.

Mom pulled up humming along to the radio. "Happy day, girl!" she said with joy in her voice. "Why do you look so glum?"

"Just feeling bad you have to drive me everywhere, you or Natalie."

"Oh, pshaw. Don't mind at all, and it gets me out of the house and out of laundry."

Candy settled into the passenger seat just as Mom said, "I hear your brother is going to Costa Rica. To surf."

Candy nodded. Should she tell Mom she was the one who encouraged him? Almost begged him? Or, would Mom care?

"Yes. It's exciting. He needs a vacation." She left it at that.

But, it came up at dinner, when Billy appeared. He had his own place, but some evenings he craved Mom's cooking, and she craved her only son. So, here he was.

He was so excited, so full of piss and vinegar, as Gramma used to say. Candy was thrilled he was happy, but Mom obviously had some reservations. She had questions.

~

Candy slammed the ten pound free weights down in place. She turned to Natalie who was spotting her. "I mean, Nat, he is thirty-two years old. He runs his own car brokerage. He's probably a millionaire. Guess I should look him up on

CANDY'S WILD RIDE

Google."

"Guess you could. And, show your mom. Would that really solve or resolve anything?"

"Probably not. She wants to believe what she wants. He is her boy, her only son. But," Candy grimaced when she replied, "what am I? Chopped liver?"

The two girls laughed at that quip, an old one from over a decade ago. Even their Jewish friends had used it. They all knew it meant the person being referred to it was lower than low. Still, it wasn't PC. Or, did that matter between friends?

Natalie tossed Candy a towel. "Come into my office. We need to discuss Cindy's list"

~

They were just about to click off Cindy's email when Connie burst in shouting. "What can I do? I want to help. And, why aren't you having the prayer vigil?"

Nat and Candy looked at each other with Frisbee eyes. Nat took a deep breath, grabbed Connie by the shoulders and shook her slightly. "First, this is Thursday. The prayer vigil is Friday. Second,' she said, "of course you can help. Maybe in a very special way."

"Oh. Got my days mixed up. Duh." Connie rubbed her ear, a habit of hers when she was nervous or embarrassed. Candy winked at Natalie and they both giggled.

"What? You're hiding something from me." Connie's face crumbled.

"Calm down, Con. We will share. But, at this point they are only suspicions, conjectures." Natalie pushed her into the stiff wood chair. "Now listen. Here's the deal." She gestured toward the computer as if it held all secrets.

Candy took over. "We have been reading Cindy's wish list. For the things she wants Billy to take to Costa Rica next week."

"So?" Connie leaned forward in the chair.

"Pickles. She wants pickles. Nathan's extra sour pickles," Nat replied. She looked deliberately at Connie's face waiting for a reaction.

"Well, she always did like spicy food." She stared at both the women. "Don't they have pickles in Costa Rica?"

"I imagine they do, but," she paused dramatically, "probably not Nathan's."

Connie still looked puzzled, shook her head, then slapped her cheeks. Just then Noelle flew in the door. Connie screamed, "Cindy is pregnant!"

The four Candy Canes hugged each other, danced around the desk in the small office, clapped, giggled and finally cried tears of joy. "We are going to be aunts!" Someone cried out.

~

Connie, Natalie and Candy elbowed each other walking through the market. Noelle had to be in class teaching Junior and Senior English, specifically Shakespeare. They knew she was devastated to be missing their shopping excursion. Missing all the fun and giggles.

"What about this?, Connie asked. "It's spicy, requires corn chips, and she can always add pickles."

The other two girls laughed. "It's not just about

spicy stuff, but about specific stuff. Press on, girls." Natalie pressed a button on her phone again to get the email list from Cindy.

"Hello, Ladies!"

"Fancy meeting you here." Nat and Candy almost said in unison.

"Just shopping for Dad and me. We are craving pasta tonight."

Natalie introduced Bill Junior to Connie who almost swooned. Candy elbowed Nat. Nat spun around as if checking out the shelves and winked at Candy.

"So, this is another Candy Cane? Are all of you beautiful?" Bill had that charm that many gorgeous men had. But, he did sound sincere. Sometimes more than his dad.

The girls chuckled, and Candy replied. "Wait until you meet all of us. Thanks for the compliment."

"Does that mean there is an ugly duckling in the group?" His laugh was deep and throaty. "I can't believe that is so."

"We think," Natalie replied, "the two who are married are the most beautiful. We will accept attractive. You will have to decide for yourself. When you meet them."

"So, when do I get to do that?"

Candy explained Noelle lives here in Newport Beach, but Cindy lives in Costa Rica, and that they were married to two brothers. Natalie wanted desperately to change the uncomfortable subject.

"That's a nifty jacket you're wearing, Bill. I'm guessing you rode your cycle here?"

"Thanks. Yes, it's one my sponsor gave to me. Boots are, too." He lifted his right foot to show them. Monograms were embellished on the outside of each boot.

Natalie and Candy exchanged glances. Connie hadn't moved since the conversation began. She was staring like a star struck preteen at Bill. How embarrassing!

"We have to do something." Candy pulled Nat aside and whispered in her ear. Nat nodded. "But what?"

Candy grabbed Connie's arm and led her away. "Nice to see you, Bill. Have a good pasta dinner."

Connie jerked her arm from Candy's in the next aisle. "What are you doing? I just met my dream man."

Candy spun her around, and in a stage whisper said, "He is *my* dream man! I met him first."

"Oh, bungled, again."

~

All the Candy Canes knew Connie had had numerous romances, all that had ended in disappointment. Natalie often wondered if Connie was too detail oriented. One time she asked Connie about that.

"I made a list. Of everything I want in a man," she said. "Is that bad? I don't want any deception like Candy had."

Trust. Where was trust? Natalie wondered. Yes, Candy had been deceived, and it cost her and her parents a great deal to remove Dev from her life, and theirs. But, she had recovered. Prayer and attending meetings for family members of alcoholics had given her more understanding. Al-Anon had helped her through it. Now, she was whole. And excited about Bill Junior as a prospect. She hoped Connie wouldn't jeopardize it. Candy had set her sights on Bill Junior that first morning she met him in the gym. Natalie thought that was a good match, until …

~

Nat and Candy transferred pickles from jars into double plastic bags with firm zippers, hoping the contents would get through customs without spilling. The smell of pickle juice would surely give it away. They also peeled off the jar labels that said Made in U.S.A. and re-stuck them to each plastic bag. Hopefully, the Costa Rican customs' officers would let them pass. Cindy really needed them.

"Especially, if she really is pg." Candy used the loose term for pregnant, but she felt in her heart she was right. Cindy *is* pregnant. They had all the various foods for Cindy and Rob scattered across Candy's mother's kitchen table when Connie tapped on the back door.

"Hey, girl! Come help. Billy is leaving tomorrow, so we need to get all this done quickly," Natalie said. "Say, why aren't you at work?"

"Taking a break. Waiting for inspiration for a new line."

"Must be fun to be a clothing designer," Candy said. "Maybe your boss could use me as a gopher. I could sure use the job."

"I wish. It would be fun to work with you every day. And, no, it's not always fun to be a designer. Only when you come up with something very unique. Much of the time it's frustrating." She smiled wanly. "You've heard of writer's block." The other girls nodded. "Well, I get designer's block. Totally stymied, no creativity." She changed the subject abruptly. "That Bill is quite a hunk, a real cutie. How did you meet him?"

"Uh, oh. Competition," Natalie winked at Candy. Candy didn't wink back.

"You have designs on him, Can? You dating?" Connie cocked her head to look directly at Candy.

"Not exactly dating. He and his dad took Nat and me out a couple of times. Dinner."

"Heavens, I don't want to impose. Maybe he has a friend?" She made it a question. A hopeful one Nat thought.

"I thought you were dating some model," Candy said.

"Male models are all so phony, so into themselves. I steer clear of them now." She caught the expressions on her friends' faces, then they started to laugh. "What's so funny?"

"Then," Natalie gasped between giggles, "you wouldn't be interested in Bill."

"What! He's a model?"

"Not the typical kind," Candy answered. "He does model clothes." She hesitated. "On motorcycles."

"You're kidding?" Connie looked astonished. "That's why he isn't all scrawny and skinny. He sure looked good in that Harley tee shirt he was wearing. Oh, well." She grabbed a plastic bag and opened a jar of pickles. "I'll help. But, could you ask him if he has any hunk friends?"

CANDY'S WILD RIDE

~

Vivian Ashford wandered into the kitchen. "How are you girls coming along? Oh, hi, Connie! So good to see you."

Another tap on the back door, and Noelle let herself in. "Just finished for the day. I had the kids in my last class acting out Macbeth. It was a treat. I'm going to entertain Braydon tonight with the video I made." She looked at the organized piles of clothing, books and food on the table. "Looks like you are almost done. Hi, Mrs. Ashford."

"Hi, Noelle. Goodness, this is a Candy Cane party. Where is Doreen? And what's that other girl's name?"

"Melanie, Mom." Candy replied.

"Doreen's in L.A. doing a show," Connie spoke up. "Modeling my gimp line. Oops, that wasn't kind, and certainly not P.C." Still, she giggled.

"Do you have a name for the line yet?" Candy asked.

"We're running a contest. The winner will receive a trunk load of clothes, her choice, and a lot of money would go to a female veterans' organization, hopefully to women who have lost limbs."

"That sounds like a terrific idea. So, how do you introduce the line now, before it has an official name?" Vivian asked.

"Right now, we are promoting it as "Unique for You." But, it's clear it is for women with compromised or missing limbs."

Billy burst into the kitchen swinging a suitcase.

"Here it is, gals, an empty one donated by Mom." He surveyed the table filled with all the stuff they had accumulated to send to Cindy. "Too much," he said. "This is not going to work."

"Of course it will." Candy glared at her brother. The other girls backed her up.

"We have it all figured out," Natalie said. "The books are thin; they will line the bottom of the case. Clothes and unmentionables – turn your head away, Billy, come next. Some maybe stuffed around other things. Food last – all in heavy double zippered bags, then in a big black trash bag to separate it from the other stuff." She stared at him. "It's gonna work, Billy. Has to."

He threw up his hands. "This is going to cost me a fortune to get through Customs."

"Oh, yeh, we forgot you are poor." Candy's sarcasm was not lost on any of them.

"Don't you have to pay to take a surfboard?" Connie's question hung in the air.

"No," he replied. "Brian, who manages the bungalows where I'll be staying, and where Cindy and Rob live, has dozens in all sizes. He will lend, or I'll rent."

The girls proceeded to load the suitcase. They wished Cindy was here to guide them. Just as they were trying to fit in the last few items, Melanie knocked on the door.

She took one look at the bulging case. "Oh, dear. I see you need me. Sorry I'm late, but aftercare at New Hope means I can't leave until every parent picks up every child." She grinned at the group. "You need me," she repeated. "You are doing this all wrong."

It was the Candy Canes' turns to throw up their arms. They stepped aside as Melanie unloaded all their hard work.

"First of all," she explained, "you've folded everything. Naw, Naw. I know there aren't many clothes, but you need to lay them out flat. With arms and legs hanging out of the suitcase until everything else is in."

"B … but?"

"I know," Melanie said, "but trust me."

"Is there anything we did right?" Candy asked.

"Absolutely. Lining the bottom with the books is perfect. Like giving the suitcase an extra bottom." She proceeded to take out pants and tops, mostly tee shirts and the sweater or two, then replace them laying the bodices of the shirts in the case with the arms hanging out. Pant legs hung out, too.

"Now," she said after flipping the pant legs and sleeves in, "give me an extra black trash bag, and blow in it."

"What?" Candy couldn't believe Melanie's request.

"Yes. Fill it with as much air as possible. To cushion the food."

The girls had a fun time blowing until Billy reminded them that there was a bike pump in the garage. Face red, from blowing and laughing, Candy went to retrieve it.

"This is much better. But, won't it take up a lot of room since it's so inflated?"

"It will deflate over several hours, but for now, it's a cushion. Trust me?" she asked again.

Bonnie Engstrom

When they finished Cindy's unmentionables and an extra pair of swim trunks for Rob had been pushed into small empty spots. Who would have guessed, Nat thought. A pair of cute underwear took up no space at all. But, they still couldn't get the suitcase closed. At least not tightly.

Melanie shushed them. "I hope the meat you are sending is sealed well and frozen? That is key."

Candy nodded, so did Natalie. They would get up early and place it on top of everything else in the case. Except the pickles. Those would be cold from the fridge, but not frozen.

"What time does Billy have to leave to catch his first plane? I want to be here to do the final packing," Melanie said. Billy looked at Melanie in a kind of weird way, Candy thought. What was going on?

After the girls had disbanded and Candy was left alone with her brother, she forced herself to ask. He was often confrontational and private, especially with his sister.

"So? What was the look you gave Melanie?"

"Oh, nothing special. I just didn't remember her that much. She's cute." Billy turned his head.

She grabbed his arm. "Why don't you ask her out. Low key, maybe a coffee date."

"I might. After I return from Costa Rica." He gave his sister a sneer. "Maybe I will meet an exotic honey there." Laughing, Billy stomped away.

~

Bill Senior and Bill Junior pushed their Styrofoam coffee cups around. Old Bill scooted his back and forth between both hands. Young Bill twisted his and moved it a few inches every now and then.

"So, Dad, I bow to your expertise. I don't think either of us have had this situation before."

"Right. It is a little weird, dad and son courting two sisters," he said, pushing his cup again. "I know they are not blood sisters, but who would know? They sure act like it."

"Yes, they are all very committed to each other." He stopped to stare at his father's hand on the squeezed coffee cup. "Do you know about Cindy? The one in Costa Rica?"

"A little. Just snippets. What?"

"She's the one all the others are supporting. They really are all committed to each other, Dad. It's a hard friendship to break through." Young Bill pushed his foam cup aside, tapped his fingers on the table and rose. "Time to go," he said with authority. He laid a bill on the table and walked to his cycle. Revving it up, he left his father in the dust.

~

Confusion. Bill Senior wasn't sure what he felt, or even if he should feel. Both Candy and Natalie were lovely women, both of them had captured his heart. Why, he asked himself, was he going in this direction? He had only been widowed three years. He had loved and adored and felt complete.

He was lonely. Grateful to have his son in his life, but wanted the companionship of a woman. In an attempt to find companionship, and with his son's encouragement, he'd joined groups. He'd tried, but had no interest in canasta, jazz, yoga, all the offerings at the senior center. He did like the

Bonnie Engstrom

Senior Fitness Class at Nat's gym. But, it was not a place to meet prospective women to court. They all wore wedding rings and, although very friendly, were just that – friendly. He felt guilty about not going to church and riding last Sunday. Was his excuse of stomach cramps acceptable? Was it believable? Even to him?

CHAPTER NINE

*B*ill gripped the hand gears tighter. The beach was a blur on his right. He knew the waves crashed and thundered, but he didn't look. Not even out of his peripheral vision. The helmet hindered. He was actually thankful for its hindrance. No need to look at the bleak horizon. He was heading south, and soon he would have to make a decision whether to stay inland to escape foraging a path through Laguna Beach and the Sawdust Festival crowds, or escape it. His destination? He wasn't sure, but he wanted to end up as far south in California as possible, without crossing into Mexico. He hated Mexico. It held devastating memories. Marsha had gotten so sick there, overcome with serious, disease infected mosquito bites. They'd had to call a doctor to come to the hotel room. No, **Puerto Vallarta** was not a fond memory.

Coronado! Maybe Coronado would raise his spirits. He pressed on and finally crossed that hideously high bridge that led to the lovely island, or was it a peninsula? He breathed a relief sigh and rode around streets off the main highway, just for fun. It was so good to be out of Newport and away from the temptation of beautiful young women. He stopped at a pancake house and filled his belly with carbs. Burping his pleasure, he jumped on his bike. This time he followed the main street all the way out to the end point, almost to the naval base. Crossing the little bridge over the bay inlet he paused to watch the ducks and their yellow babies. Seeing new life gave him hope.

He checked in to the Loew's Coronado Bay Resort, asked for a luxury room overlooking water of any kind. Got it. Threw himself down on the expensive bed in the cabana and fell sound asleep. His own snoring woke him up.

~

"Dad!" Bill Junior yelled into the receiver of the land line in his condo kitchen. He hung up in frustration and dialed again. Bill Senior's cell phone went to voice mail for the third time. Where had Dad gone? Without telling him. The only time that had happened before was when Mom was dying.

He jammed the instrument back in the receiving holder and called Nat's Gym.

"Sorry, Bill, I have no idea where your father is. Is it an emergency? Has he done this before?"

"No and no. That's why I'm concerned. Not like him."

"Is his car there? He didn't come into the gym this morning. But," she muttered, "you probably know that since I think I saw you here."

CANDY'S WILD RIDE

"Car is here, but," he hesitated, "Harley isn't." Bill ran his long fingers through his thick hair. Where had that crazy man gone? "That's when I got concerned, when he didn't show up at your place, your gym. He is usually pretty prompt. I thought maybe he wasn't feeling well and I would find him in the hot tub when I got home. But, no deal."

He hung up his kitchen phone just as his cell beeped.

~

"Sorry, Son. Needed to get away. Why don't you hop on your bike and join me?"

"Just glad you are all right, Dad, but can't. I have a shoot tomorrow, a big promotion for Harley duds.

"Dad, what's bothering you?"

"Not sure I even know." Bill Junior sensed his dad was pacing, something he often did when talking on the phone, even the one on the kitchen counter. Bill Junior waited. Finally, a big sigh and the sound of munching on chips.

"Try. I did minor in psych in college," Bill Junior quipped. "Woman?"

"More like 'women,'" was the reply. "Too young."

"You mean Natalie? Or, Candy?"

"Spot on. I could in a moment bed either one."

"DAD!"

"I know – feeling my old age. But, those girls are beautiful, real treats. Hard to get them out of my head. And, they both seem to like me okay."

"Like isn't love, Dad. They are both at least thirty years younger than you. Too young." Bill gulped. "You need to find a companion your own age, maybe to even be a substitute mom to me. Someone you can trust who isn't a gold-digger."

"You saying you don't trust those girls? They seem so much above board. Christians, too."

"I don't think they have ulterior motives, but they are young and probably impressionable."

He slammed down the phone, called the Loew's and secured a room near his dad's.

~

Candy was concerned. Nat had shared her conversation with Bill Junior.

"Do you think he's okay?" Candy wasn't sure exactly why she was so worried about Old Bill, but she kept remembering the sensation in her knees when she had wrapped her arms around him on the cycle. She hadn't expected it, was surprised. She had designs on Young Bill. She was so over older guys after Dev. Then why did Old Bill claim a part of her heart?

~

Billy complained loudly about the weight of the extra suitcase. He had spent the night at his mom's because it was closer to Orange County Airport that his own digs in Dana Point. Expecting it to at least have rotating wheels, he was disappointed and, well, angry. What had those silly Candy Cane girls been thinking? At least he could check his bag and the extra one curbside, but he wasn't sure about the Customs situation. Would he have to schlep it?

"Stop yelling, Billy." Mom had put on her command face. "You are taking an old case of your dad's. It was the best option. It's super large and so scuffed up already it won't matter if you decide to leave it there." She turned away to flip bacon strips in the skillet. "He doesn't need it anymore."

Billy felt bad when he heard her sniff and reach for a tissue. Dad had died suddenly several years ago. He had hoped by now she would have at least started socializing with people her own age. Instead, although she did belong to a garden club, she spent a lot of her time with his sister and her Candy Cane friends. Working in her recently planted vegetable garden seemed to be therapeutic, and he and Candy relished her salads of fresh greens. But, both of them hoped she would take up more social hobbies.

Vivian Ashford flipped more bacon and stirred scrambled eggs. "Sorry. I really want you to have a good trip."

Billy wolfed down his eggs and rose to the beeping horn of the taxi. "Thanks, Mom. I will." He gave her an extra strong hug, and she started to cry, her body shaking in his arms. "Take care of sis, and" he added, "yourself. Pray for me." It was an afterthought.

~

Candy heard the commotion in the kitchen and the taxi horn. How had she awakened so late? She rushed to the door to give Billy a hug, but he was gone. She knew if he had a safe trip and got through Customs all right, he would have fun. She counted on it. Mom told her Melanie tapped on the door at five a.m. and put the frozen meats in the bag. Thank goodness someone was organized.

That battered up suitcase would be a lifeline for Cindy and Rob. Had she remembered to tell Billy to slide a big American dollar into a hand of a Costa Rican Customs official?

~

Bill Junior flung a towel handed to him by a pool attendant on the back of a chaise. He wasn't sure Dad even knew he was there. He'd finished his photo shoot yesterday, succumbed to an hour of informal modeling with women fawning over him, jumped on his bike and headed south. The feeling of breeze blasting his face revived him. He skimmed by the Pacific and its brilliant colors. Orange, pink and faded blue filled the horizon. If he hadn't been is such a hurry to meet Dad, he would have stopped. Still, the sound of crashing waves assaulted his ears, even through the helmet. It was a sound he had grown up with.

"Dad?"

"Oh, you're here." Bill Senior's voice sounded sad, and lonely.

"I'm here. You okay? What is wrong?" He didn't want to intimidate Dad, but he sure wanted to know. Dad had told him in that phone conversation that women, or maybe woman, was what was bugging him. Not an easy topic to discuss with your widowed fifty-plus father, but maybe necessary, maybe time. God does give second chances, doesn't He?

~

Billy passed through Customs in Costa Rica palming a one hundred dollar U.S. bill into a middle-aged gray-haired uniformed man's hand. The battered brown suitcase had flown down the chute, so different from the luggage carousels in the states. It landed with a loud whoosh, but it didn't burst open. He hefted it and put it on one of the provided carts. The U.S. currency did the deed.

~

"Gotta go home. Sorry." Bill Senior grabbed his overnight case, and left his son in the dust. He checked out via the TV, jumped on his bike and headed north. Bill Junior was still sprawled on a chaise by the pool. He had fallen asleep soundly, a result of his long day before. He reached over to pat Dad on his arm and found air. Maybe he had gone to the bathroom, or to the pool bar for a drink. He waited. Twenty minutes was a reasonable time, wasn't it?

The cutsie girl with the pixie haircut smiled broadly at him. "He checked out."

What was wrong with Dad? In the three years they had been living together since his mother's death, they shared everything. He grabbed his Bible and went back to the chaise. Hoping for answers, he opened at random to James 1 and skimmed down to verse five. He texted it to Dad.

~

"What are you doing here?" Candy didn't mean to sound confrontational, but she was surprised.

"Had to see you. Can I come in?"

Candy opened the door. Why was he in motorcycle gear and clothes? Didn't he have a proper car?

At her gesture he removed his leather jacket. Threw it on the sofa haphazardly. Striker sniffed it. Approved, and moved away to slump down next to the fireplace, even though it was summer and no fire. Snuggling his legs under him, the dog settled in a position of doggie comfort.

Maybe, Candy thought, she should take a clue from Striker. Just get comfy and wait.

~

Bill rubbed his chin. What a fool he was. When she shared the story of her former marriage, he understood. Although, he didn't like it. Couldn't she see he was nothing like Dev the Drunk as she called him? He even tried to sway her by explaining how in biblical times the males were usually decades older than the women they either courted or married. He knew she wasn't convinced, but he'd tried. Maybe he should grow a beard, or at least a goatee. It was the "in thing" right now. Even if it aged him, it would make him look more hip.

They had talked for an hour, until her mother returned from shopping. Vivian Ashford was very courteous, actually gracious. She gave him a pretty smile, offered coffee and presented a plate of homemade cookies. He'd passed. Now, he wondered, had he offended her by refusing? He certainly realized where Candy got her looks. That old song about a pretty woman came to mind. The mom was very attractive. What was he thinking?

Leaning close toward the mirror above his fancy bathroom sink he peered again at his chin. He covered it with his palms trying to imagine what it would look like with a trim beard, although he rather liked the idea of a goatee. Maybe sideburns, too. Then, he closed his eyes and drifted back to his conversation with Candy. What was it she had said about Natalie? He couldn't remember the exact words. Gosh, was he that old? No, he'd been flustered. Something about Nat being disappointed, but said in a way that indicated she was interested in him. Him, Bill Lord. Senior.

Aw, what had he done?

~

What had she done? Candy couldn't decide whether to run to Mom for advice, or call Nat and confess, or hug Striker who was sniffing the gloves Bill had left on the sofa. Striker won. She rubbed behind his right ear and he sighed. She picked up the errant gloves, stuffed them in her purse to take to the gym tomorrow and ran to the kitchen for Mom advice.

Vivian Ashford was washing fresh lettuce from her garden. With fury. Her mother shook it so hard water splashed all over the kitchen and on Candy's face.

"Mom! What are you doing?"

"Just venting in my own way."

Candy felt her jaw drop and her mouth hang open. She knew what it was about. Bill Senior. Old. Thirty years older than she. She decided to be strong, and realistic. But, when she spoke, her words came out in a warble.

"Mom, I know why you're worried. It's not like that."

"Not what I heard," Vivian replied. "I wasn't eavesdropping, but the kitchen is only steps away from the living room." She sighed. Bitterness crept into her voice. "He is an old man, Candy, who rides a motorcycle. Too much **Déjà vu**."

Candy threw on a jacket, grabbed her mom's

keys and ran to her mom's car. She had shaken the keys, and Mom nodded her head. Turning the key in the ignition, she was conflicted. Should she go to Nat's, or to Bill's? Then, she realized she didn't know where Bill lived.

Vivian ate her salad alone.

~

Natalie was punching the keypad on the gym's outer door. A new installment Bill had ordered as part of his involvement in her gym. It was much more secure than the old padlock and key version, and made the place look more professional. She had had to request all the original gym members return their keys. She wondered why she had even given those out. Maybe as a way to show she trusted them? Still, it had been naïve and dumb, and definitely not business like.

When she heard the final beep from the keypad, she also heard a soft beep from a car horn.

Candy. In her mother's car. What?

~

"I screwed up." Candy hugged Nat who pushed her to arm length and peered into her eyes.

"Why are you shaking? What happened? Share."

"Bill came to me. Confession time, he said. He was very distraught." Candy looked Natalie square in the face. "Can you accept this?"

Natalie had no clue, but lifted her shoulders, plastered a smile on her face and said, "Yes."

"I think he has fallen in love with me. Me!"

CHAPTER TEN

"Chips! You packed ten bags of chips." Billy's voice boomed through the invisible phone lines.

It was a California area code, so Candy answered. Hoping. Wrong move.

"I spent a small fortune transporting corn chips to Costa Rica? What were you thinking?"

"Calm down, Billy." Candy sucked in a breath. "How was your flight?" Wasn't that the first question one asked when hearing from someone who had recently landed? She regretted the question. Billy was in no mood to be polite.

It was his turn to suck in a breath. "Sis, I can't believe you sent chips. I bribed the Customs guy a hundred smackers to let that suitcase through without opening it. A hundred bucks!"

She should have been prepared, even been expecting this diatribe. Billy had always been this way. In fact, she was puzzled he'd never asked to see what was in the suitcase. She had given him a cursory list so if anything was missing he would know. But, she'd only listed chips, not how many bags of them.

"Did the pickles get through okay?" She held her breath waiting for another barrage of anger.

"Yeh. No leakage. She was, is, very appreciative. Seems she *is* expecting, so I guess the pickles and chips really are important." He paused for maybe thirty seconds, then said more calmly, "She and Rob really appreciated the books. They took them out of the case and actually prayed over them. What're they for, anyway?"

"For their mission, Billy. For to build a church."

"Oh," he said. "God work."

"Billy, what did you think of Dev? Other than his drinking problem?" She had changed the subject abruptly. The questions jumped out of her mouth unbidden. "His age, I mean."

"He was okay. His age didn't bother me, made him sort of like a father figure. Except for the drinking. THAT bothered me. Why?"

"Just wondering."

"You head over heels for another older guy?" He seemed to be waiting for an answer, but didn't get one. "Sis, what are you up to? Does this guy have a name? Is that who you were attached to on the cycle the night I saw you?"

"N – no. That was his son."

"So, he has a son your age. Interesting." He dragged the word out in four syllables. "Why don't you go for him? Or, isn't he flush enough?"

"They are both very 'flush,' as you put it." She paused to collect her thoughts, and decided since she had brought the subject up, and for once he was being patient, Billy deserved an explanation.

She explained how Natalie really had her sights set on the father, how the man had invested in her gym to help make it more profitable, also how Logan Lovejoy and Darrell Day had worked with him before and trusted him – at least financially. "He's almost a Newport legend, I guess."

"I will ask again, Can. Does this legend have a name?"

"Bill, like you." She giggled. "Bill Lord. Senior," she added.

Billy's whistle almost shattered her eardrum. "Guess you've heard of him." She tried to sound nonchalant. Didn't work.

"*The* Bill Lord? *The* Bill Lord?" he repeated. "Wow, sis, you sure pick them." She heard him click his tongue. Then, "Do you have any idea who Mr. Lord really is? Any at all?"

"Uh, he's a very nice man with good manners. He's considerate, kind, courteous and handsome, and … He says he thinks he's in love with me.

"Striker likes him." Her voice sounded weak even to herself. "Dontcha, Strike?" The dog lumbered up to the coffee table where her purse was sitting open. He stuck his long snout in and pulled out one of Bill's riding gloves and laid it on her knee. "You should see what the Striker just did, Billy." She explained about Bill accidently leaving his gloves yesterday.

"Was Mom home?" he demanded. His voice was loud.

"Yes, don't worry. She even offered him coffee and cookies."

"Humph. Just like her."

Candy was getting tired of this conversation. It was probably costing someone a fortune. She hoped not Cindy and Rob. But before she could say goodbye, Billy chimed in again.

"Sis, you have a pee-rob-lem."

She whispered, "So?"

"I heard the man is still in mourning for his late wife, and … his son is a spoiled brat."

"Says who?" The assessment of the two Bills angered her. "Bill Junior is a very nice man devoted to his father."

"Swishy?"

"No!" Her turn to shout. "In fact, Mr. Know It All, young Bill is the one I had my eye on, and Nat was, maybe still is, attracted to Bill Senior. So there." She was tempted to slam down the phone, but Billy had actually carried on a conversation with her; something he seldom did. She hoped the call was on his nickel. Maybe a lot of them.

~

She hung her purse on a hook in the hallway with the glove back inside. Striker hadn't wanted to give it up, but finally did when she threw him a treat. Yuk! Doggie slobber. She wiped the glove off with a paper towel, then wrapped it in a dry one and stuck it in her purse next to its companion. Frustrated after her conversation with Billy she knew she needed exercise to burn off her anger.

CANDY'S WILD RIDE

Pulling on her athletic shoes she decided a walk would feel better than working out at Nat's Gym. Fresh air always did the trick. She sauntered down San Juaquin Hills Road, knowing it would be a long climb back up when she was exhausted. She would worry about that then. As she approached Rogers Gardens, she could smell the heady scent of flowers. Although she couldn't power walk in there, it would be a nice diversion. All the colors and floral scents should raise her spirits. She wove her way through the crowded parking lot and because she was looking beyond, almost bumped into a motorcycle. Actually, two. The Bills were here. But, why? Neither of them seemed like gardeners, but who would know? She followed the path past the latest plantings to the Garden Room. That's where the orchids were that Mom loved so much. She was entering the side door to the covered area when she heard her name.

~

Bill Junior touched her arm. She turned half around as shivers rushed through her body. "Oh, hi!" Did that sound normal? "What are you doing here? You have a garden?" Her questions sounded lame, but since they had already been spoken, she clamped her mouth shut and smiled. She couldn't take them back.

"No," he replied. "No garden. Wish we had the space and expertise for one."

"Then what is the reason for your being here?" Why couldn't she keep her errant mouth shut? Why, Lord, am I in this uncomfortable situation?

"Mom's grave," he said simply. No inflection,

just a statement. "Every year this time. The day she died. It's special to us."

"Oh, how nice." She couldn't think of anything else to say when Natalie appeared.

"What are you doing here?" Another lame question.

"Came with the Bills to support them." She looked curiously at Candy. "You didn't know? To put flowers on Marsha's grave. Wanna come?"

Candy shook her head. She hadn't been invited. And, she was sure it would be awkward.

Bill Senior held up a plant and waved it in front of her face. "Do you think your mother would like this? To add to her veggie garden?" Candy couldn't identify it. Seemed like an herb of some kind.

"She probably would, but why?"

"Because I want to, and," he hesitated as if not sure to go on, "because she was so accepting of my company the other night."

"How nice. Thanks. I'm sure she would love any plants."

He started to thrust it into her hands, then pulled it back. "Sorry. I should deliver it myself."

"Great. Because I am on a walk, so it would be difficult to carry." She released a giggle, turned and walked away. "Enjoy the evening."

What had just happened there? Candy tilted her head back and looked at the dark sky. Rain was predicted for tonight, but it was only late afternoon. The clouds above Newport seemed to move swiftly – big billowy white ones with dark outlines. Newport's clouds blew in from the Pacific Ocean due south. Tonight they seemed to be moving faster.

CANDY'S WILD RIDE

Maybe she should get home. She had no raingear, no umbrella. Southern Californians seldom carried them. Go figure.

~

Bill, Bill and Natalie were drenched, caught in a downpour. Natalie had a hoodie on, but the men had left their helmets at their cycles. She wasn't sure why she was here. Was she so desperate for a boyfriend, for male companionship, that she would even accompany him to a grave? Or, maybe it was 'them,' not him. Clinging to each of their arms, she was confused.

It had been weird running into Candy at Roger's. But, the whole day had been weird. When she'd arrived at five-forty-five to open the gym, Bill Senior was pacing on the curb. He'd followed her in after she punched in the new door code. Gave her a quick hug and marched to a treadmill. She hoped the hug was just friendly now that they were business associates. After he had spent forty-five minutes on the treadmill and Bill Junior had taken her Zumba class, the two of them ganged up on her. Or, it seemed so. Maybe she was a little paranoid.

~

"Why did you agree to go to the cemetery with them?" Candy even questioned her own question, but she needed to know. And, she worried about Nat. After all, having been married, even to Dev the Drunk, she felt like she should look out for Natalie who was more naïve, less worldly than her. Who was she kidding? She remembered her conversation with Billy. She was no expert in men.

"It was sad. And special." Candy heard

heartache in Nat's voice.

"Tell me."

"Two grown up men cried, then smiled."

"They both loved that woman. Obviously."

~

Candy stewed around, flung clothes against the wall of her bedroom and over the chair. She picked up the sandals she had worn that night when the Bills drove up on their cycles. Not the best choice for riding a motorcycle, but she hadn't known. She threw them in the trash. Good riddance to strange memories. Time to go job seeking again. Her money was running out.

Melanie had suggested, even pressured her, to try the preschool. "But, I am not good with little kids." Candy made that clear, but Melanie said there were other options. So, today she marched in to New Hope Preschool and met with Dana the director. She was lucky to get an appointment; blessed, Melanie said. The place was so cheery; a red heart rug on the floor, pictures of adorable children everywhere, a woman named Lorrie greeting her like a long lost friend. She felt comfortable. That had been a long time in coming.

"This is not right for me," Candy said. She actually did feel comfortable talking with Ms. Dana, but she felt uncomfortable taking up her time. Little children were not her future. She was sure.

~

"Welcome, Candace." Ms. Dana shifted some papers, then looked Candy straight in the face. No, the eyes. "I see from your letter and resume you believe you are not teacher material."

CANDY'S WILD RIDE

Candy nodded and felt her ridiculous pendant earrings jangle against her jaw. Why on earth had she worn those? To make a statement? Surely, teachers who worked with little children didn't adorn themselves that way. Hopefully, Ms. Dana would see that.

Ms. Dana rubbed a finger across one eyebrow, leaned forward and peered again at Candy. "You're sure?" She asked in a gentle manner, not challenging.

"Pretty sure. Actually, quite sure. I've never worked with kids. I find them scary." There, she'd said it. She fumbled with the zipper of the purse on her lap. "I've never been around many; never babysat when I was a teen."

"Mmm. Sounds to me as if *you* are scared." Ms. Dana set the resume aside, clasped her hands and, again, looked Candy straight in the face. "Melanie has great faith in you … as a friend and a Christian woman."

Candy nodded. This interview was not going as she had planned. She had hoped the director would tell her she wasn't qualified, no deal. She was only doing it to appease Melanie.

"I understand you are divorced. But, I'm not supposed to discuss that. However, you did emphasize that several times in your application letter, as well as your resume. Reason?"

Candy nodded. Hopefully, that would put her resume in the slush pile and she could leave this stressful situation.

"That," Dana said, "is not a deal breaker. At least three of our teachers are or have been divorced. Myself, also," she said with authority.

"Really?"

"Yes." It was a simple statement.

"Oh. I thought that wasn't acceptable in a Christian school." She fidgeted some more. What was happening here?

"The only thing important is, hopefully, you are a Christian. But," Dana cleared her throat, "legally that isn't supposed to matter. Still, it is rewarding that you are." She picked up a paper Candy hadn't noticed before. "This is a letter of introduction from Melanie. Tell me about the Candy Canes."

For the next twenty minutes Candy opened her heart. She explained about the high school swim team and how the girls were all still best friends. How they still supported each other in so many ways. She even got into a tangent about Cindy and Rob being missionaries in Costa Rica and how they sent Bible study books and food to them. Finally, she clasped her hands on her shaking legs. "Sorry. I went off," she said. She reached for a tissue on Dana's desk and dabbed her eyes.

"You have a very special and blessed relationship." She handed Candy another tissue. "Can you start tomorrow?"

~

"You are doing what?" Natalie's voice rose to a high pitch.

"I am going to work at New Hope Preschool. Can you believe it?"

Nat shook her head. "No. But, I believe God led you there." Her encouraging grin sealed the deal for Candy. The hug helped a lot, too.

CANDY'S WILD RIDE

"I'm scared, Nat. All I've ever done is retail. And, I hated it. This is so out of my league."

"Then, why did she hire you? She must have seen something special, even redeeming."

"I'm still not sure what I will be doing. I think she said something about starting with supervising kids on the playground. I think I could do that." She grinned at Nat. "But, I still have reservations. Please pray I don't yell at them. I walked through the campus with her today. The children are so adorable. They ran up to her for hugs. 'Ms. Dana, Ms. Dana' they said. 'Do you love me?' How can I compete with that?"

"You don't have to. She isn't asking you to. Just be yourself." Natalie hugged Candy. Tomorrow she would be gainfully employed, making about nine dollars an hour.

~

Bill Senior was both appalled and confused. He and Candy had met at Nat's Gym at six a.m., and she shared her new employment. What was she thinking? She had never had children or been a mother. How could she do this?

After she told him her exciting news and did some bench presses, she ran off. "Gotta shower and get ready for work," she'd said. "First day on the job. Wish me luck." She had raised a hand; he raised one back.

~

She walked into the New Hope office in tennies and a comfortable workout outfit. Seemed right for the job.

Ms. Dana and Ms. Lorrie greeted her, and Dana

took her hand and led her around to every classroom. Some of the children were doing crafts, and some were singing. All were adorable.

A bell rang, and Dana said, "This is your cue. Assist on the playground." Then she left.

Tawnie, the teacher of the four year olds, turned to her, said "Hi," and told her to take three kids to potty. What?

~

"You what?" Natalie started to giggle uncontrollably. She coughed and sputtered. She had a vision of Candy wiping little bottoms and holding small hands under the faucet. Candy pounded her on the back.

"Really, Nat. That's what all the adults do at the preschool. Even Dana sometimes. We take turns. I'm sure Melanie has done her share of potty time. Part of the deal."

"I just can't … I just can't … see you doing it." She gasped and giggled again, then sucked in a deep breath.

"Hey, girl. I'm grateful for the job." Candy gently slapped Nat on the shoulder. "And," she continued with emphasis, "it's a great place to work. Everyone is kind and cheerful, and best of all Christian. And," she rolled her eyes, "there are always treats in the office. Today it was Ms. Lorrie's chocolate chip macadamia nut cookies. Homemade." She grinned sheepishly. "I took two."

~

Bill Senior called. She wasn't sure how he got her cell number. Probably Nat leaked it.

Certainly not Mom who was against anyone

older than thirty. Too bad, Mom.

"And to what do I owe this honor?" She made an attempt to be light.

"Wanted to learn how your first day with the little ones was." She was sure he was grinning on his end of the call.

"It was great, terrific even." She paused to give him the full effect. "I did a lot of potty duty. And, gorged on cookies."

"You pilfered from the kids' lunches?"

"No, silly. The cookies were in the office for everyone to take. Homemade. Chocolate chip. Yum." That should put a bee in his bonnet. Or helmet.

"Oh. Dinner tonight?" He sounded so hopeful. "Maybe something low-key like Pei Wei? On my cycle."

"I hate to refuse. But, I really am very tired after all that potty duty." She almost choked trying not to giggle. "I'm sure you understand."

"Sure. Sort of." She could hear the disappointment in his voice.

"Sonny not available?" Why had she used that moniker for Bill Junior? However, Bill Senior did call him that.

"No, he has a date." That was all he said. No information.

"Good for him." But, she wondered.

"Nat didn't tell you?"

"No. We only saw each other for a few minutes when I stopped into the gym after work. She was busy." Yeh, right. Why did Nat hide the date with Bill Junior from her? The relationships with the

Bills was getting complicated.

Her phone buzzed again. Oops, she still had it on silence as a concession for during work. Actually, she liked the low buzz better than the chime. "Hi, Con. I saw your name come up.

"Sure. You are welcome to borrow anything. But what on earth would I have you'd want? You are the clothing designer, so you must have scads of gorgeous things." She paused to listen to Connie's chatter. "Why do you need a long wool scarf? It's almost summer."

"Who with?" Noelle the English teacher would probably slap her for such inappropriate grammar. But, Connie on a motorcycle? No, couldn't be.

"Which Bill?" She had guessed right. Almost.

CHAPTER ELEVEN

Candy left the long wool scarf on the porch. She wasn't sure she wanted to see Connie. She felt as if Nat and Connie had been a little underhanded. Not to mention Bill Senior. What was going on? The Bill situation was getting out of hand. Maybe she was making too much of it. But, Big Bill did make it very clear the other day that he cared for her. But, how? In what way? Had he said specifically? No. It had all been inference. Clothed in ambiguity. What did "I care more than you know." mean? Or, "If I had a choice, I would make a move." What did he mean if he had a choice? He does. And I want it.

You do, Bill, you do! She wanted to scream. At him. But, he either wasn't listening to his heart, or he was horribly confused. She was, too. She felt herself falling hard for Bill Senior, the one Natalie had in her sights, the one her mother was against because of his age. Now, even Bill Junior was unavailable since Connie was hugging onto his back on a motorcycle. The Bill situation was more than complicated. She decided to try very hard to set it aside, but couldn't. She needed her Candy Cane sister, the strong one.

Apparently it took a long time for a call to go through via California to Costa Rica. Cindy answered after numerous rings. She was so insightful. "Trouble?" she said. It was a strange way to answer the phone, but so very Cindy. Somehow she knew.

Candy did her best to explain, but since Cindy didn't know either of the Bills, it spilled out diluted and jumbled. She tried to go through the whole scenario from the beginning, how Big Bill made a play for Nat and practically insisted in investing in her gym; how he brought his son, Young Bill, into the mix and she, Candy, had thought they might click. She told her about the cycle rides and dinner, and giggling how Nat had consumed so many oysters. Cindy finally laughed. But, she had been listening intently in silence before Candy shared that escapade.

"Wait," Candy said. "There's more." She explained about running into Young Bill in the supermarket when they were shopping for pickles and chips. That part of the scenario gave Cindy the giggles again. Until Candy told her about Connie's date tonight.

"What!" She thought Cindy would magically morph or mutate through the phone lines, that's how upset she sounded. "Connie wouldn't do that," she finally said with resolve. "She wouldn't." Candy heard a sigh and pause. "She did, didn't she?

CANDY'S WILD RIDE

Didn't honor the Candy Cane sisters promise."

"Yeh, almost like the one doctors take … to do no harm, and," Candy added, "to honor and respect and support each other and never steal another's boyfriend." The day they had graduated from Vista del Mar, they had made a solemn pact, a promise, a treaty to each other. They didn't do the blood thing like so many teen boys did, but clasped hands and prayed together, but they promised to honor their special commitment. Yes, they were young, and perhaps naïve, Candy thought, but all Christians, they intended to honor it. Until now, when Connie hadn't.

~

Connie twisted Candy's scarf around her neck and jumped on the back of Bill's cycle. She wrapped her arms around his torso and clung hard to the softness of the leather jacket. Her hands were clasped around his chest, and her breath blew on the back of his neck. What, she wondered, was she doing here?

They pulled up to a restaurant she didn't recognize. He parked the cycle and made a big play of helping her off. "Thanks," she said. "I've ridden before, and I'm okay."

That seemed to impress him, and he did a little bow when he removed his helmet and locked hers and his under the cycle's seat. She had to remind herself this was Bill Junior, the son. The gorgeous one. The model with the intentional, scruffy five o'clock shadow impersonating a Hawaii 5-0 actor. What was she thinking? She had just given Nat and Candy a sermon about how she loathed male models. Now she was dating one.

"Where are we?" Connie asked. Should she be wary? This restaurant was off the beaten track. It was a funky little Italian one nestled in a small inlet next to the water. But, obviously popular, because about twenty people were sitting outside waiting on benches. She hoped the food was good. They had taken Newport Boulevard, the main street of the Peninsula, then cut through a few side streets she wasn't familiar with. But, the smells coming from the door of the cottage-type place were tantalizing. Her nose actually wiggled. Maybe Sabatino's Lido Shipyard Sausage Company was okay. Should be with such a long name.

Bill grabbed the lapels of his leather jacket, shook it a bit from his frame and strode into the entry to give his name. A cutsie young woman with red streaks in her brown hair led them to a small secluded table in a corner. Her fake diamond studs glittered in the low light. "Hi, handsome," She winked as she tossed menus on the starched white tablecloth. "We always serve antipasta first." She signaled to a female server who plunked down a narrow dish laden with small bites of meat and olives and peppers. Cutsie had ignored Connie, then turned back almost as an afterthought and said, "Oh, Sweetie, hi to you, too. Welcome."

Connie grinned and started to pick at the peppers on the dish. She wondered if Bill had been here numerous times before. Although the hostess didn't suggest that, the fact they had been seated immediately did. So? Whatever. Didn't matter. She was with Mr. Gorgeous.

CANDY'S WILD RIDE

~

Candy heard a long, loud sigh from Cindy's end. Finally, Cindy said, "I don't know what I can do. She is her own person, but has never had the same level of commitment the rest of us have. Maybe it's that creative streak. Want me to call her, or email her?"

Candy felt guilty. She was calling Cindy thousands of miles away asking her to help with a situation right under her nose. She changed the subject. She was getting good at that. "So, how are the chips and pickles?" She laughed and waited.

"Probing, are you?" Cindy asked.

"Not really. Billy told me. I am sorry if he ruined your surprise."

Cindy roared with laughter. "Oops. Gotta run to bathroom. Call you later."

~

Connie felt her eyes get donut-sized. Tall, angular, thin but buff Mr. Gorgeous was attacking a huge plate of sausage and peppers. Like he hadn't eaten in a month.

She decided to be diplomatic. "Good, huh?"

"Great, the best. How's your ravioli?"

"Delicious, but way too much for me." She took another small bite and rolled her eyes in pleasure. "I will need a doggie bag for sure."

She couldn't resist any longer. "How can you eat so much and still pose and look so – so lean?"

His answer startled her. She put down her fork. What?

"I joined your friend Nat's gym, and I work out every day. However," he said, "I believe it's genetic. Dad is pretty slim and buff. For his age," he added with a grin. "Grandpa Lord was always slender, even in his nineties. Guess we are just blessed."

"Lucky you. Being in the fashion design business, I have to be careful."

"You don't have to model your designs, do you?"

"Not often. But, I do attend a lot of events, and I am supposed to look glam."

Bill reached his hand across the table and touched hers. "You are more than glam, Connie. You are naturally beautiful."

Heat creeped up her neck. Was this man for real? Even in her business, surrounded by media and other designers and models, both male and female, no one had ever said she was "'naturally beautiful.'" She smiled, squeezed his hand and said, "Thank you. That's one of the best compliments I've ever had."

The words would cover her like a fuzzy blanket when she tried to get to sleep tonight. Sleep had come hard lately.

CHAPTER TWELVE

*B*ill Senior tossed and pulled the sheet over his face. Daylight Saving Time was the pits. Light filtered in through the shutters in his bedroom. Maybe forty minutes more of sleep would help. He couldn't get her out of his mind. Both the young girls were beautiful, but there was something about *her*. Like they had an affinity for each other. They had only met that once in her living room. Still, he'd felt the connection. She had smiled at him and lowered her head and blushed. Was he crazy? He was certainly confused. He needed to talk with his only confidant.

"Son? You still in Coronado?"

"You're here? In bed in the condo?" Why hadn't he heard him? Maybe he was getting hard of hearing, old. "You up for coffee?" He set down the phone, showered quickly and jumped on his cycle. Starbucks was only ten minutes away.

~

Bill Junior was shocked. He stared at his dad's shaking hands wrapped around the paper cup. "You sure?"

"No, not one hundred percent, but close." Bill Senior squeezed his eyes closed. His son was sure he saw moisture under his dad's lashes. "Do you think she'll go out with me? Would it be weird if I asked her?"

Young Bill felt his shoulders quivering from hard contained laughter. "Naw, Dad. I think it would be great."

"Ya think?" Dad seemed so uncertain, like a school boy worried about his first date. Actually, when Bill Junior thought about it, that's what it was. First date in over thirty years.

"Dad," he hesitated to ask, but did. "Do you think this feeling has just happened after we visited Mom's grave?"

"Maybe. A little, but …"

"But what? You scared?"

"Yes, and no." He leaned forward, his elbows on the round table. "Those girls are both adorable, classy and beautiful. But, I feel like they are my children." He looked Bill in the eyes. "Not love interests, not appropriate. Either one would be a wonderful daughter in law to take care of me in my old age."

Bill grabbed his dad's hand and squeezed it. "Then do it, Dad. Call her. At least try."

~

Vivian Ashford couldn't believe she was meeting Bill Lord for coffee. Surely, he wanted to talk about Candy and ask her permission to court her. Or, was that an ancient term?

She straightened the jacket of her coral pantsuit and slipped on open-toed sandals. Thank goodness she had gotten a pedicure the other day. Her big toes sparkled with the rhinestones along the tips of their burgundy polish. Kay, whom she had dubbed the best manicurist in all creation, had accented her thumbs and ring fingers with the same sparkles. Why Vivian had succumbed to such extravagance she wasn't sure. Maybe a gift to herself since it was just a few weeks away from Mothers' Day?

She picked up the ringing phone. Candy always called on the landline knowing her mom wasn't used to the cell phone. "Hi, honey. What's up?"

"Gonna be late, Mom. I still have two little guys whose parents haven't picked them up yet."

"That's okay. I have to run an errand. Leftover lasagna in the micro." She couldn't, just couldn't, tell Candy where she was going and with whom. Too embarrassing, maybe even subversive. Definitely not right.

~

Bill ordered the new fancy caramel latte for her and placed it carefully in front of her. "I didn't ask. Sorry."

"Yum. Smells good. Thanks." She studied his handsome face. Why was she here? Would he be her next son in law? He certainly had more class than the Dev guy, but he was about the same age. She couldn't contain herself any longer. "Why am I here, Bill? You need my permission to date Candy?"

He slapped the table and both of their cups

bounced. His sudden laughter surprised her. She shrunk back in her chair, and it bumped into the one behind her. She turned to the man in that chair to apologize when Bill grabbed her hand.

"No, Viv. May I call you that?" He didn't wait for a response, but just kept talking. What he said made her knees feel weak and shaky, and her tummy got a tight knot.

~

"I did it, Son. I asked her out." Bill Junior almost felt his dad's nervousness coming through the phone. He inhaled and exhaled a deep "Whew."

"Good for you, Dad. I'm proud of you. So, what did she say? How did she react?" He was dying to know.

"She seemed shocked at first, then flattered. 'I didn't expect this.' She said." He paused for a breath. "But, finally, she agreed to see me another time. Once. As long as it is our secret for now."

~

Vivian drove home with shaky hands on the steering wheel. Bill had insisted on following her at least half way. She was grateful for that, but didn't want Candy to hear the roar of a cycle close to her house. She waved when they were getting close, and he waved back and turned around. Was that a kiss he blew? Heavens, this is all so sudden.

"Hi, Mom. Where did you go? Oh, you look lovely. Special occasion all dressed up?"

"Not really, but thanks. Just a coffee with a friend." Vivian prayed she could pull off the deception. Candy was pretty intuitive. Still, how would she even guess?

She changed into sweats, cleansed the makeup off her face and settled into the sofa with a fresh cup of coffee from the carafe. How could she ever tell Candy that the man her daughter thought was in love with her was really in love with her mother?

~

Cindy called back. "So sorry, but I had one of those pre-baby runs."

"Still not barfing, I hope?" Candy hoped her question wasn't offensive.

"Nope. Just need to run to the bathroom a lot now that baby is bigger, and" she sighed, "pressing on my bladder." She stopped to giggle. "Now, what's up?"

Candy filled her in about the two Bills and the motorcycles, as well as her own new job and reiterated the Connie situation. "Confusing, isn't it?"

"Yes. But, maybe a little less so from my vantage point. Sometimes, when one isn't involved personally, it's easier to figure out."

"Okay, girl, start figuring."

"Do you remember my gut feelings about things?" Cindy asked.

"Yes, and you had a good track record with them. What is your gut telling you now? Or, is baby in the way?"

"Baby's only in the way when I eat too much." Candy heard Cindy's delightful laugh, then her friend went on. "From what you've told me, just a guess though, both Bills are players. I don't sense a serious romantic streak in either. Dad Bill is lonely and kind of egotistically proud to be seen with beautiful young women half his age. Son Bill isn't ready to get serious about anyone, wants to play the field. Does that sound right so far?"

"Sort of, unfortunately." Candy found it hard to contain her disappointment. "Maybe Nat and I should play scarce."

"Yeh, the absence makes the heart grow fonder thing. Or," she continued, "if it doesn't, then give it up. At least you have a chance to know one way or the other."

CHAPTER THIRTEEN

"We have to stop meeting like this. It's too deceptive." Vivian touched Bill's hand with a sparkly fingertip. They had decided to meet during the day when Candy was working at the preschool. They were sitting in a random coffee shop in Laguna where they figured no other patrons would know them. Still, it made Vivian uncomfortable, like a teenager sneaking out of the house so her parents wouldn't know.

"Sonny knows," he said matter of factly.

"You don't think he'd tell one of the girls, do you?" she asked.

Bill rubbed his still clean-shaven chin. What had he been thinking when he got the idea for a beard? Facial hair had always made him itchy. "I hope not," he said, "but he is pretty excited about us." He said "us" very tenderly. "You think it's time to tell Candy?"

"Maybe. Guess I'll have to work up the nerve

to do it." She pulled her hand back and started to fold and refold the brown paper napkin on her lap.

"Would it help if I was there, too?" He leaned forward and smiled, then shoved his chair back and scooted in next to her on the bench. He laid one hand over both of hers and wrapped his free arm around her shoulders and squeezed it. She nodded.

"It's settled. What time does she usually get home?"

~

Candy was shaking so hard she could hardly steer. Mom had handed her car keys over, gave her a hug and said, "Go to your friends."

She was not about to go to Connie. She was still miffed at her for going out with Bill Junior. Nat was the obvious one. She prayed she would be home.

Natalie was just parking her car in her designated covered space next to her condo. Candy beeped her horn and slid into a guest space, jumped out of the car and ran to her friend with tears streaming down her cheeks.

"What's wrong? What's happened. Is Cindy all right? Baby okay?"

Candy nodded and collapsed in Nat's arms. "It's us, Nat. He doesn't care about either of us. Neither of them do." She gulped and mopped her face with the tissue Natalie had dug out of her purse.

"Oh." She dragged out the exclamation. "Then who?"

Candy started sobbing again. "It's Mom. My mom."

CANDY'S WILD RIDE

Natalie often started to giggle when she was nervous. It was a terrible habit she regularly had to control in devastating situations, like funerals. It had almost happened when Doreen had her accident. Now, she felt as if someone had died. At least a dream had.

She held her nose to hold in the giggles. But when she started to hiccup loudly, both she and Candy burst into giggles. Candy ran to the bathroom. When she returned she announced, "Almost wet my pants! Yikes, Nat. What are we going to do?"

"We," she stated firmly, "are going to do nothing. You are going to go home and hug your mom." She looked Candy straight in the eyes. "We can't coerce other people's feelings. I'm sure Bill and your mom didn't plan to fall for each other. Besides, it may be a temporary infatuation. Wait and see."

They had stumbled up the outside stairs to Natalie's little condo and were huddled on the sofa. At least Candy was with crumpled tissues strewn around her. Natalie was sitting erect with hands lightly clasped on her lap.

"How can you be so calm?" Candy asked. "He was the one you originally had eyes for." She heard the anger in her voice.

"I've been praying for direction. I felt something was a little off … with both Bills. Young Bill wants to play the field. I don't think he's ready for a serious relationship. Old Bill is lonely and wants stability, comfort, familiarity. That's what your mom can give him. Besides," she added, "she's a very attractive lady. Notice I said lady, not woman." She smiled at her friend who had seemed to calm down somewhat. "Now, go. Go home, hug your mom and tell her you are happy for her. And, if Bill is still there, hug him, too."

"That's what Cindy said, too. About lonely and playing the field. You know what I mean." She hugged Natalie, cleaned up her tissue mess and walked out praying for courage.

~

Bill and Mom were waiting for her, arms linked. Was she going to be in Melanie's situation with a stepfather? Surely, Bill would be one she could admire, not like the horrible Bruce Walker, Melanie's stepdad. She pasted on a grin and ran to them hugging both together.

A lot of sighing went on. Then, both Mom and Bill started to speak at the same time. Mom won, as moms always do. Candy chuckled.

"Thank you, Candace." Mom used her formal name. That meant something, didn't it?

Candy smiled through veiled tears. She really was happy for Mom to find someone to love, and love her back. She realized she had apparently misread Bill's comments to her the day he was over. Or, maybe he had changed his mind. She had often been told she was the spitting image of her mother. But, she would never make her mother's famous chocolate chip cookies. No, God had put His hand on this couple. She, Candy, had misunderstood His intentions.

"So, what now?" She blinked hard and waited

for their response. This time Bill spoke.

"We are taking it slow, Candy. Your mother is an exceptional woman, but I don't want either of us to rush into anything. At our age we don't have a lot of time, but we have time to reflect and get to know each other better. That okay with you?"

"Perfectly. Now you two cuddle on the couch and watch a flick. I am going to my room to fill out some paperwork for work. By next week I may be a teacher with my own classroom."

She heard the cheers as she raced up the stairs to her room. She reminded herself of Cindy's often repeated phrase, "God is good … all the time."

CHAPTER FOURTEEN
Five Months Later

Candy stood up tall. She could do this. She twisted the waist of her gown and made sure a tissue was stuffed in the sleeve. All she could think about at this moment was Daddy. She knew in her heart he would be pleased his beloved Vivian would have a happy life ahead of her.

"Daddy, please, send me a sign."

Just then her cell rang. She had forgotten to turn it to silent. She didn't recognize the number, but in her nervousness she picked it up. "Hello?" No answer, just silence. Starting to tuck it back in her waistband, she felt it buzz again. This time she had remembered to put it on silent. This was getting annoying. She decided to give it one more try and pushed the green accept call button. She was sure she heard a kiss.

Just then she heard a commotion. Billy?

"Get out of here, now!" Her brother's voice

rang loud in her ears. Who was he yelling at?

The lovely wedding of Mom and Bill was over. She had glided down the aisle in the soft lavender gown, even accepted and held Mom's beautiful bouquet designed by Love In Bloom Floral, by Braydon himself. The man was a genius at wedding bouquets. The yelling escalated. She heard Billy's voice loudly. Then Bill Junior's. Two men screaming. What was going on?

Natalie was holding court, waving her hands. Or, at least trying to divert the situation. Connie gripped Young Bill's arm. She looked terrified.

Candy rushed over to the men who were arguing. Fists were raised. Voices were almost vulgar. This was supposed to be a time of celebration with dancing and cake cutting and congratulatory speeches. What was happening? She stared in unbelief.

Brother Billy was in the face of another man. Young Bill, the groom's son, had fists raised to use them. The third man stood stone still. Devin? Her ex? Dev the Drunk?

How could this be?

Candy couldn't move. Her body was in lock down. What on earth was Devin doing here, at her mother's wedding reception? Before she had the nerve to speak, he did.

"I came back, Candy. I am whole. I want you back." He walked toward her with hands held out and palms up. Almost like when she praised in church on Sunday mornings.

Her first instinct was to run.

She practically sprinted past a group of guests

seated at one of the long tables in the Rogers Gardens Farmhouse Restaurant. She pushed and shoved through a cluster of women admiring the wedding cake. Mom and Bill Senior were chatting with the Days and the Lovejoys, the women smiling and the men laughing. Must have been some joke. She prayed Mom wouldn't see Devin. That would surely spoil this otherwise perfect day for her.

The restaurant had just opened several weeks ago, so she couldn't quite get her bearings. Where was the parking lot? She dashed almost headlong into a huge pot overflowing with purple flowers and stubbed her toe. So much for the expensive satin shoe. Where, oh, where was the parking lot? She gasped for breath and felt wetness on her cheeks. She had to get out of there – now. She heard voices behind her. Then her name called. Masculine? Bill Junior? No, older than his. She ran into the first open door. Maybe there was someplace she could hide. She was in The Garden Room, the partially covered area filled with indoor plants. She spotted the gorgeous orchids her mother liked so much. Braydon had put trailing orchids in Mom's bouquet. The arrangement was stunning. Why was she thinking about that? Her mind was all muddled and confused. She needed to escape. How could she possibly believe Devin? It had only been two years since their divorce. He couldn't be sober, could he? After this fiasco was over, she would call Rob in Costa Rica and ask. He had been sober now for almost seven years. He would know, he would advise her.

She searched for something to hide behind.

CANDY'S WILD RIDE

There was a large arrangement of pottery. Squatting down, the hem of her delicate lavender dress skimmed the dusty packed dirt floor. She visualized carrying the dirty garment into Newport Hills Cleaners.

Her name – called again. This time she was sure it was Devin. She couldn't breathe.

"Candy? My beautiful Candy Cane, where are you? Please come out and talk."

He had always dubbed her with that moniker. It brought back so many memories … dancing in the moonlight, snuggling beside him in bed … drinking – his. No, she refused to go there again. "Too late, Dev," she whispered to herself. "Too late." But why was her heart beating so wildly?

Finally, the voices drifted off in the distance. She rose and tip-toed. She was close to the entrance next to the parking lot. She almost made it outside, then the voices got closer. Spying the gift shop still open, maybe in hopes wedding guests would wander in and purchase something extravagant. She swooshed into it. She had always loved this place. She and Mom came every Fall to purchase wonderful Radko Christmas ornaments. One year the designer was present, so they stood in line and got signed ones for an extra price. But, so worth it.

Holding up her skirt, she quietly skimmed past a lovely display of glass and a large statue of a Buddha. Ugh! She knew there were other statues somewhere of St. Francis the patron saint of birds and animals. But, the Buddha unnerved her. She spied a chair nestled into a section of home decorating items. It was so far back in the gift shop she felt safe to sit in it. For a moment. To catch her breath. Then she heard voices again. Several male ones she couldn't distinguish, but Natalie's lilting one was obvious.

"Candy, it's me. It's really okay. Please come out and be part of this wonderful party."

Candy guessed Nat didn't actually know where she was, or she would have ventured into the gift shop to look for her. She kept very still, and very quiet. Finally, the voices drifted away. This was her cue. The gift shop was just inside the entrance, and the parking lot was just outside of that. If only she could find what she wanted.

~

Mom's car was there, but she didn't have the keys. The two Bill's cycles were parked on either side of it. They always left them locked. Next to Old Bill's, her new stepfather, was the gorgeous red mini-Harley he had given Mom as a wedding gift. Had she actually ridden it here on her wedding day? Candy didn't stop to contemplate when she noticed the keys dangling from the ignition. How could this be that Bill and Mom were so negligent? Maybe Mom did ride it here to please Bill. After all, she had a special room to change into at Rogers Gardens before they posed for their wedding pictures. Maybe Mom, who often forgot things, left the keys in.

Candy approached the cute red cycle with caution. She hoped the security at Rogers Gardens wasn't videoing her. What if it was? She was a bonafide part of the wedding. She jumped on the seat, revved the motor and prayed Mom would forgive her. She had to get out of here and away from Devin.

Candy sped up San Juaquin Hills Drive to Newport Coast. She could feel the skirts of her gown flapping in the wind. It was so exhilarating, so freeing. She had left Dev behind.

But she had nowhere to go.

~

She heard sirens. Why were sirens so close? She prayed for them to help whomever they were coming for. She couldn't move her legs. Her beautiful lavender Maid of Honor gown was crumpled under her, getting dirty. Actually, dirtier, after the hem dragged on the ground in the Garden Room. She chuckled to herself thinking about how embarrassing it will be to carry it into Newport Hills Cleaners and explain what the stains are. Ow, her arm hurt. Trying to move it, she couldn't. Maybe it was hindered by the bunched up gown. So sleepy. *Gotta close my eyes.*

Angels? Who was calling her name? Were God's angels male or female? Sounded like both.

"Candy, Candy. Open your eyes. Smile at me." Was that Dev's voice? She hated Dev. He almost destroyed her life. And her faith. The female voice sounded like Natalie. Even though she hurt, she smiled. She barely focused through slit eyelids, but the man who lifted her onto some kind of flat bed-like thing was gorgeous. What Connie would probably call a hunk.

~

"Wh … where am I?" She could barely hear her voice. Why was she asking? The wedding reception wasn't over yet. The cake hadn't been cut. She tried to see what was happening, but her eyes wouldn't focus. Images of people moving around her upset her. "Get away from me! Leave me alone!" She twisted and struggled, but they kept touching her, then lifting her. She wanted their hands off her, but she had no control.

She was sure she heard her mother and Natalie whispering. Their voices were so faint she could only catch a few words. What were they talking about? Broken? What was? He ... changed ... healed. Who?

Two gentle hands touched her left arm. With effort she got their owners' faces almost in focus. "Mom? Nat? Why aren't you dancing at your wedding? Where's Bill?" Both women smiled and Mom shrugged. Suddenly, Candy remembered loud arguing. The Bills,

Junior and her brother. Then Devin, her ex, calm. Why wasn't he frightened by them?

Mom's voice competed with the ringing in her ears. "Later, dear. We will explain later."

"When you're up to it," Natalie said. At least that's what Candy believed she said. She tried to shake the cobwebs out of her head, but there was a stiff obstruction around her neck. And, she couldn't twist her right arm. Trapped! She was trapped. But, why would Mom do that?

"Good afternoon, lovely ladies! Sorry to interrupt, but I need to wheel this gorgeous girl to X-ray." Who was this man? She could see through her blurry vision he must be handsome, and he wore a wrinkled green top.

CANDY'S WILD RIDE

"She still a little foggy?" he asked. Mom and Nat nodded. She could see that much. "Might be the pain meds," he said. "Plus the trauma. This may take a while," he explained. "X-rays, maybe a CT scan, definitely a cast if the bone is broken." He looked at Vivian; Candy could see that. "You the mom? She have any broken bones as a child? Any head trauma?"

Mom shook her head. Why were tears on her cheeks? This was her wedding day, special to Big Bill. Where was he?

Mr. Handsome suggested Mom and Nat go home. "This may take several hours. By the way, Madam, you look beautiful. You, too, young lady. Special occasion?"

Nat choked through tears. "Wedding." Then she pointed to Vivian. "Hers."

The young man's eyebrows shot up about two stories. Then, he grinned.

CHAPTER FIFTEEN

Candy used her card key in her left hand to open the big red gate and shuffled into the preschool office. Miss Lorrie grinned at her and winked. A parent came in with a child clutching her jeans. She heard the mother speak to Lorrie about how Aaron was scared to come to school today. Candy was about to enter Ms. Dana's office in hopes to get out of teaching today. Her arm really hurt, and she was embarrassed about the bruises on her face. Before she knocked on the director's door a small voice spoke more loudly than usual and tiny arms wrapped around her leg.

"Miss Candy, Miss Candy!" She felt the tug of his hands on her pants.

"Good morning, Aaron! How are you today?"

"I good, now you here. Where you been, Miss Candy? I missed you."

Aaron was one of her favorite students. He was so adorable with his tousled black hair and pouty little mouth. She learned that until she became one of his teachers, he had cried every day. He was a small child for his age, and Dana had comforted him enough every day that he had gone back into class. The school policy was to never force or insist a child return to class, but in Aaron's case his parents both worked long hours, and he would have been subjected to a babysitting service if not at the preschool. So, everyone tried to make Aaron comfortable and feel welcome and special. Until Candy came, it had been a daily trial.

Candy bent down and hugged the child as best she could with the clumsy cast on her arm.

"What that?" he asked pointing to her pink cast.

"Broken."

"It hurt?"

"Sometimes. But, you made it feel better."

"Good. I go to class now. See you." He skipped off ignoring his mother and running to Room Three.

Candy changed her mind about asking for time off.

~

Devin had bought her a car.

The man was full of surprises. The new Dev.

Her emotions were all mixed up in her heart, and her memories were scrambled like a kaleidoscope, jumbled and constantly changing. Her thoughts jumped from questioning why she had been so attracted to Bill Senior, older like Devin, to why did she even listen to Dev's explanations of how he had changed. She desperately wanted to believe him, and if she did, would she even want to go back to him? She simply didn't know. She had been so young when they'd married, yet felt ancient when she struggled through the divorce process. Confused? You betcha, as Gramps used to say.

She opened the silver car door and slid into the passenger seat. With effort she lifted her cast-wrapped arm and waved a finger over the ignition button. Such new-fangled stuff! As long as the actual key was on her person, the door lock opened and the car started. Shifting gears was the biggest problem. But, it had that new gearshift that only required a touch to go from drive to reverse and a slight touch between them for park. Dev had spared no expense, and according to him he could afford the luxurious coupe. She was still mystified at herself for accepting it. He had begged, and she believed it was a way he felt he could redeem himself. When she finally nodded through tears, he looked so relieved, and so proud. And, she desperately needed a car.

Mom had been appalled and angry. But Bill calmed her down and explained how important the healing process was for Dev's male ego. Rob described the AA steps to her on the phone, too. Finally, she quietly accepted that Dev was back in Candy's life. For how long no one was sure – not Candy, not Mom and not even Dev. Mom also said sarcastically, "He at least owes it to you."

One day when Vivian was checking her bank account online, which she only did occasionally, she discovered huge cash deposits during the last three months. She called the bank's 800 number, but since the money deposited had been cash there was no way to trace it. She, Candy and Bill surmised it was from Devin. He seemed to be constantly trying to make up for his sins, as Mom called them. Candy reminded her Dev had never hurt her physically, just her heart, and of course himself. He had been so unhappy within himself that he tried to drown in alcohol. Now, he was sober and extremely successful. He was, as he put it, blessed.

The architectural firm he had worked for took him back. His creativity was outstanding according to his former manager, Jeremy Cox, who was now a partner in the company. Immediately assigned to design several city buildings in Northern California, actually an entire complex that included retail businesses and a hotel and a public library, he was back on the map again. His concept for the project was innovative and unique and gained acclaim for the firm. And him? He made a lot of money. But, would all that last? That was Vivian's big concern, as well as how Candy would deal with a new and revised Devin. When he started showing up in church on Sundays and joined the men's group with the Bills, she was more accepting. What really clinched it for her was when he invited Billy to the Wednesday evening group, and Billy accepted. Her son had shied away from anything faith based for years, mainly because of Devin and his behavior. Now he was signing up to be a greeter before services. Vivian could be caught mumbling "Praise the Lord" while making dinner, or even when doing laundry. Bill would put his arms around her and squeeze, pecking her on the neck.

Candy was grateful for her mother's happiness

with Bill. Why had she ever had an attraction to him? He was kind and caring, and best of all comfortably wealthy. They often socialized with the Lovejoys and the Days since the men were old friends. Life had finally been good to Mom. It was the younger generation that seemed in limbo.

Candy struggled constantly about her feelings for Devin. Natalie confided in her that she found Bill Junior extremely attractive – who wouldn't? – but her heart didn't flutter when she was around him. He still met his dad at the gym several times each week. "A little father, son, bonding," Bill Senior said. Bill Junior just laughed.

"Who does make your heart flutter, girl? Anyone?" Candy was sitting in Nat's office as they read Cindy's last email together. When she asked her friend the question, she noticed Natalie turned crimson. The color crept up from her jawline to her nose. What? There must be someone. "You embarrassed to share? Do any of the other Candy Canes know?"

Nat shook her head. "Secret," she said. "He doesn't know I exist." Nat was blinking rapidly.

"Nat, I can keep a secret. Honest." Should she pressure her friend? Of all the Candy Canes they were the closest. Cindy was in another country, Connie was so involved in the design firm and now had her own line Winning Designs, Doreen was modeling for Connie, Noelle was married, even Melanie was so involved in teaching now at the preschool she seldom socialized with the other girls.

"Too personal."

"Let's see," Candy started to tick off on her

fingers whom would be too personal to her that Nat wouldn't share. "Not Bill Junior. We've already established that. Not Dev, certainly not him, I hope. Not that cute barista? He's way too young for you, but he is a looker. Maybe the paramedic who rescued me? Or, the grinning guy who took me to X-ray in the hospital? He was pretty special, but I think he wore a wedding ring.

"Oh, one of Rob's surfing dude bros? Nick or Brad? They are both AA and very successful in business. I want you to be matched up with someone who is successful and can take care of you. Financial success is important I've learned. Also, age." She paused and screwed up her rubber face, the one the other girls always made fun of. "I know I'm not the best example of that. If I decide to leap with my heart, I may be pushing Dev's wheelchair in twenty years. The growing old together baffles me, but it's definitely something to consider."

Natalie shook her head no at every suggestion. Finally, she said, "He's my age. Or close. Close to you, too."

A light bulb exploded in her brain. Mom had even mentioned the possibility. She took Natalie by the shoulders and turned her from the computer screen to face her. "Oh, my gosh! Billy? My bro?"

Natalie looked miserable, but she nodded, and a single tear rolled down a rosy cheek.

"Well, we have to rectify this," Candy exclaimed with a gleeful voice. "The man is an idiot, even though he is my brother. He is extremely successful, he is just a few years older than you and me, he's handsome … at least I think so. But, he is dense. He lives in La La Land. What can we do?"

"Don't know. Don't even think he notices me. I have given up." Poor Natalie sounded so downtrodden. What had she tried? Candy asked.

"You know me," Nat said. "I try not to be too forward. But, I did ask him to dance at your mom's wedding. Then, you know what broke lose when the Dev situation happened. And," she paused, "when you took off on your wild ride."

"Yeh, I messed everything up, didn't I?"

"Not your fault. Things happened you had no control over."

"I should have had more control. I reacted when I should have stood my ground and addressed the situation. If I had, I wouldn't be wearing this pink cast now. I am so sorry."

Natalie blinked and shrugged. Candy figured she was forgiven, but she needed to help her friend. And her clueless brother.

~

"Mom, here's the deal. Any ideas?" Candy was so frustrated with Billy she hoped Mom would come up with something to get him and Natalie together. At least for one date.

"I've given up," Mom said, "but, maybe Bill has an idea."

Bill did. He loved being presented with the latest romance dilemma. He was a romantic at heart. "I will put on my thinking cap and pray. God will give me ideas."

Candy laughed gratefully. She was absolved, maybe.

CANDY'S WILD RIDE

Since Bill was a major investor in Nat's Gym, he had an excuse to promote it. Candy wondered if his idea would take hold. The next morning instead of jumping on the treadmill, he rapped on the glass insert of Nat's office door. She was sending out group reminders to pay this month's membership. "Yes? Hi, Bill. What brings you?"

"I've been thinking we need to offer a special promotion, something optional, a bonus members can pay extra for," he said. "I have an idea."

~

Natalie liked the idea, but she was scared. She was still a strong swimmer. But, surfing? The balance thing and catching just the right wave without being pulled under frightened her. Could she learn? Bill said he would find a teacher for her, a perfect teacher. She had to trust him. Swimming in a pool wasn't scary, but swimming in the ocean was.

"Got your lessons all planned." His voice sounded excited. "You need to get fitted for a wetsuit and meet him Thursday morning at five." He told her where to go for the fitting. It was all paid for. She was to meet the instructor at The Point, the most notoriously difficult surfing in Newport. She reminded herself she had to trust.

She showed up at the designated time. Hovered by her car. Who would the instructor be? She half expected some forty-year-old guy with tattoos and a lecherous grin. Then, she heard her name.

"Natalie? That you?"

Billy? Candy's brother? No. Couldn't be.

"Hi. Didn't know it would be you. Not my

idea," she said as an apology.

"I didn't either, but so nice it is." He lugged two surf boards and grinned at her. "Let's get started."

He smiled, he actually smiled, and didn't hesitate that his student was her. Natalie adjusted the new wetsuit over her old striped Candy Cane swimsuit and followed Billy into the water.

~

"Where has she been?" Billy asked Candy during dinner at Mom's and Bill's house.

"Been there all the time." She glared at him over the dinner table. "You clueless?"

He shook his head in denial. She was sure he didn't want to admit his attraction for Natalie. But, once a long time ago, he had mentioned her. After all, he did take her to the prom.

"Maybe you should join Nat's Gym." Candy couldn't believe the words were spoken by Mom. Bill nodded his head. What was going on?

"Maybe I will," Billy managed to say with a mouth full of pot roast. "Need to have a place to work out some of the kinks. I hate those big crowed gyms."

~

Candy knew she was in denial. Her heart beat faster every time Devin was near, but she refused to admit it. She had heard of couples divorcing, then remarrying years later. The ones she knew of were mostly Mom's age. She reminded herself she was still young, and there were a lot of fish in the sea. Still, her heart wouldn't obey.

The short amount of time she had spent

attending Al-Anon during the strenuous divorce had given her insight. Not forgiveness, just more understanding of Dev's problems. She really wanted to believe he had changed. She had burdened Natalie way too much already. Could she trust Melanie? Of course she could. She had taken the Candy Cane oath. Maybe a chat over coffee would help.

Now that both had reached teacher status, neither had to stay regularly for aftercare. She offered to drive, not thinking about how her luxurious new car would affect the other girl. She had gotten so used to it after several weeks she almost took it for granted. "But, how can you drive with your arm in 'that thing'?" Melanie's eyebrows raised forming little pyramids. Candy realized since she always parked around the side of the building Melanie never paid much attention. Probably thought Mom was still chauffeuring her.

Candy laughed. "You'll see." She patted the outside pocket of her shoulder purse just to be sure her remote key was there. As she approached the car door she barely touched the handle and it clicked open.

"Wow! Cool!" Melanie slid into the passenger seat and ran a finger along the wood detail on the door. "You strike it rich, or something?"

"That's what I want to talk with you about."

~

Candy drove to Riverside Avenue. She was craving a chocolate croissant. The women settled at a small table with their treats and piping hot coffee. Melanie had a raisin brioche. C'est Si Bon never seemed to change, just get better. Candy dabbed chocolate from the corner of her lips with a paper napkin, then cleared her throat. Melanie said, "Well?"

"No, I didn't strike it rich, Mel. The car was a gift, a guilt gift, for years of hurt and anger." She filled Melanie in on her former marriage to Dev the Drunk, although she didn't call him that to Mel. She told her about the several years of divorce proceedings and how expensive they were, draining what little funds she had, and the financial burden on her parents. She'd always wondered if the travesty had contributed to Dad's heart failure. No, she couldn't go there. She needed to get advice about what to do now that Dev had changed. Hopefully.

Melanie's delicate hand rested on Candy's. Her eyes filled with sympathy and moisture.
Finally, she spoke. "You know, don't you, that I used to party a lot?" Candy tilted her head and shrugged. "That's partly why I ran into Doreen. I was beering it up with some friends. I don't think I was drunk, or maybe I was. Anyway, I got distracted, made an illegal left turn, and rammed into the front of her little car, and ... ruined her life." She stared deliberately at Candy. "I know I'm forgiven, both by Doreen and God. It's me I can't forgive."

Candy laid her other hand on top of Melanie's. "Mel, you really do need to forgive yourself. Look at far you've come, and look at how special Doreen's life is now. I seriously doubt if she would have had a modeling career without the accident and her injury."

"I know. She probably could have, but might not have pursued it. Still, it's for gimp clothes. And," she added, "praise the Lord for the Candy Canes, and for Connie coming up with the idea for that special fashion line and hiring Doreen. You have no idea what you all mean to me." She dabbed at her eyes. Thank goodness for paper napkins.

Candy chuckled. "Now, give me some feedback, a gut opinion, please."

"Speaking of gut, what is yours telling you about your former husband?"

"My gut tells me one thing, and my heart another." Candy blinked rapidly. "I … might still love him." Her next words were barely a whisper, and Melanie had to strain to hear them. "I really was in love with him, even during his worst moments. But, I knew our marriage was destroyed. I couldn't deal with it, or him. Mom was collapsing under the strain of Dad dying and my calling her almost every night for advice and support. It was awful. Dev refused to acknowledge his problem, refused to get help." She looked up at Melanie finally. "I think he's in a good place now. Totally AA."

"Idea, Can. Have you discussed this with Rob? I remember he is AA and very successful. Committed."

"I did, sort of. I was so flustered when I called him a while ago, when Dev came back and caused all that ruckus at the wedding. I was very angry and, like you, did a stupid thing. In my case running." She held up her pink-wrapped arm, then laughed.

"Maybe I need to call him again. Maybe I need to grow up. After all, I was a married woman who should have been able to figure out options to help my husband." She paused and fiddled with the now crumpled napkin resting on the table. "I was so young." She shoved her chair back and stood. "Let's get out of here," she said, then leaned into Melanie's ear. "I was only twenty-one. Should have listened to Mom. But, she and Dad married right out of high school, so that was my ammunition."

CHAPTER SIXTEEN

Rob's voice was like music to her ears. Such a kind man. He suggested he call Devin and have a heart-to-heart. Candy loved that idea, got her off the hook. She gave him Dev's cell number.

Rob, wonderful Rob. No wonder he was Cindy's hero. It was hard for Candy to even imagine him drunk, but she supposed he got very depressed after learning he had MS. Still, he was a kind and caring man. Took after his dad, she suspected. After he reassured her he believed Devin was truly committed to turning his life around, and to Candy, she felt much better. She thanked him profusely and could visualize the smile on his face and the shrug of his shoulders. She congratulated him on his forthcoming fatherhood. He laughed with joy. Then, he put Cindy on the line.

They had gotten pregnant in July, just one month after their wedding. Mom and Bill had married in September. So, Cindy was just four months along. That meant the baby would be born sometime in the spring. April? Nice month. Candy was glad to hear she was over the morning sickness part. They prayed together for Cindy, the baby and for her decision about Devin.

"I always liked him, Can. Thought he was a nice guy who obviously adored you," Cindy said with conviction.

"Yeh. He did, and still does. It's a tough call, Cind. Heart says one thing, brain another." Then she asked the loaded question. "Do you know yet what sex the baby will be?"

"Not yet. Could, but putting it off. My wonderful life with Rob has been full of surprises. But, I know everyone is dying to know. Maybe soon." Candy heard the excitement in Cindy's voice. All the other Candy Canes wanted to plan a big virtual shower for Cindy and Rob, but for a boy or girl?

"Oh," Cindy blurted out. "We have a friend coming to learn surfing from Brian soon. He's an AA friend of Rob's from Orange County. He's offered to bring stuff to us if you can get it to him in an empty suitcase. Good thing about guys," she laughed. "They don't pack much." Then, she asked, "How is the Billy, Nat, situation? Or, should I call it a romance?"

"Never sure with Billy boy, or even Nat. Those two are non-committal. Sorry I don't have any details to share." Cindy promised to send the email address of the guy going soon to Costa Rica. The Candy Canes would fill another empty suitcase with whatever the young Lovejoys needed.

CANDY'S WILD RIDE

When the email came through, its address was dcinOC@yahoo.com. Why did it look familiar?

~

Devin was struggling. Not with alcoholism – he had that under control. It was his heart. He finally got up the nerve to call Vivian. She agreed to meet him and said she would bring Bill.

She settled in the now familiar corner table at the coffee house and laughed. "This is becoming more than a habit," she said. "I think it's time to carve my name in the table."

Bill laughed, too. Devin looked curiously at both of them. Private joke?

Vivian reached across the table and laid her hand on Devin's arm. "I need to be sure you understand something, Dev." She used her former son-in-law's nickname and noticed he seemed to relax a little. "I never hated you, just your behavior and how it affected Candy. I did what I did to save my daughter."

He nodded his head and produced a crooked smile. "I know, Vivian. I hated myself, too." He cleared his throat and covered her hand still on his arm with his own. "I love her. Never stopped. She was the best thing ever to happen to me – ever."

Vivian smile warmly. "I know. You have no family, and in a way I suppose we became your anchor."

"Yes, and I blew it. Maybe I tried too hard and got so anxious about us I used alcohol to unwind. But, of course, it didn't. It cost me my marriage and my job."

"But, I heard you got your old job back?" She

made the comment a question.

"I have been very blessed. My former manager is now a partner in the firm. He never gave up on me. I recently designed a huge project that has received acclaim." He grinned proudly. "The final construction should be completed in a few months."

Bill high-fived Devin, and Vivian used the brown paper napkin to wipe her eyes. "I'm so glad for you. You've had a struggle and risen up from the ashes."

"I want her back, Vivian. And, I am hoping for your blessing. I've learned that anything worth having is worth fighting for. I am ready to fight for Candy."

~

Devin stared at the computer screen. An email from Candy? The email address it came from was hers. The subject line said 'Trip.' Aw, she didn't know this was his new email addy. After reading through it, he understood. Cindy had sent this address to Candy, and Cindy probably got it from Brian the manager of the bungalows. Candy had started her post with *Hello, Friend*. She said she learned he lived in Orange County and was planning a trip to Costa Rica. Could he take a suitcase full of things for Cindy and Rob Lovejoy?

He wrote back he'd be glad to. He was leaving in five days, so how will they get the luggage to him? Could they meet somewhere centrally? He waited for her reply.

~

Again the Candy Canes were loading an old suitcase Vivian had given them. A few devotional

CANDY'S WILD RIDE

books lay on the bottom and one about what to expect from a newborn, like no sleep! Noelle laughed at that one, and Melanie grinned. Doreen had a free afternoon, and they were all thrilled she could participate. "Don't you at least have a fitting or something?" Natalie asked.

"Madam Designer gave me the day off." She chuckled. "The slave driver!" They all laughed at her quip, all knowing Connie drove only herself, staying up all night sometimes to put finishing touches on a design. She had finally selected a name for her designs. The women encouraged her to at least incorporate part of her name, Connie Winfield. All were thrilled when she chose Winning Designs.

They got to work with Melanie supervising the packing again. This time instead of loading corn chips in zippered plastic bags, they stuffed the bags with tubes of lotion. Some of it was a special sunscreen, and some was special cream for soothing tight skin and reducing stretch marks. "Baby stuff is big business," Doreen exclaimed. "I know it's a third world country, but surely they have some comparable stuff there."

"It's actually quite advanced in the pregnancy and baby stuff. Great docs and lovely hospital in San Jose. But, Cindy fell in love with some of this stuff online and ordered it and had it sent to Nat's gym. So, here we are!"

"So, who's taking it? You ever learn his name?" Noelle asked.

"He goes by, of all things, Will."

"Another one? At least it's not Bill." They all giggled getting a kick out of that.

Bonnie Engstrom

Candy loaded the suitcase in her lovely new car. They had decided to have Will pick it up at Nat's Gym. Bill Senior insisted on coming along. Who knew what this Will person would be like, and Bill didn't like the girls meeting with some unknown alone. Especially, now that Candy was officially his stepdaughter. He jumped on his cycle and waved. He would meet them there.

He got there before them, parked the Harley and decided to wait outside. Now that he was an investor, he had the combination to the lock, but chose not to use it.

A dark blue BMW coupe pulled up and parked down the street a ways. The man approached him with long strides. "Hello, Bill. What are you doing here?"

"Devin? You are the Will going to Costa Rica? My word, I would never have guessed." He peered into Devin's face almost nose to nose. "Does Candy know?"

Devin shook his head. "Wanted to surprise her. Not sure if that was wise now."

"Me, either." Bill shook his head. "Prepare yourself for a tirade."

"Yeh. Guess I'd better." He shoved his hands in his pockets and slumped. "Dumb move on my part."

"Let's pray about it." Bill threw his strong arm over Devin's shoulders and leaned close to him. "Dear God, We are trusting you in this situation. We know you are a God who forgives our mistakes, a God who rights the wrongs. Let us feel your comfort and security, and, please, give Candy acceptance of Devin's deception, even though it wasn't deliberate. He trusted You. In Your Mighty Name. Amen"

~

Candy banged her fist on the coffee table, then slammed her bare feet there and crossed her ankles. Striker lumbered over and rested his jaw on her leg. She patted his head and tried to ignore the slobber. After all, he was showing sympathy, doggie style.

"Calm down, Can. Maybe this was a good thing." Natalie's face took on a serious look to match the tone of her voice.

"Yes, look at it as a positive, God's will. Oops, sorry about the 'will' part." Doreen said.

"I agree." This comment from Noelle matched a nod from Melanie. All the Candy Canes were around her, except design driven Connie. She had a deadline, but sent prayers. Of course, Cindy wasn't there – probably snuggled in bed with her hero Rob in Costa Rica.

"Ugh! How could I be so stupid? I should have figured out from his initials. But no way would I have thought he'd be going to Costa Rica – to surf. Or, learn to." She thumped her heels on the table, and Striker ambled away. Probably too much drama for an old gentle dog.

"Enough! Enough!" Vivian practically stomped into the room. Candy could tell she was upset. "This trauma drama has to stop." She looked directly at Candy whose eyes lit up with anger. Fury green Vivian used to call them when Candy was a tot and had a temper tantrum. She actually had hazel eyes, the kind that changed color based on light or emotion. "It's time to grow up, Candy. A man loves you, a mature man who has turned his life around … because of you." She put her hands on her hips and turned to leave the room.

Candy started to cry. "Wait, Mom. How do you know this?" she managed to choke out.

"I just do. Trust me. And, trust God. HE knows what He's doing, and He knows all about Devin. Who, by the way, is waiting in his car outside." Then she turned and left, mumbling about laundry.

EPILOGUE
December

Candy stared dreamily at the filmy dress hooked over the closet door on a satin hanger. Connie had designed it similar to Cindy's, at her request, although shorter and pale frosty green, not white. Even on the hanger the sheer overskirt billowed making the gown look like it was floating. She wondered if she was overdoing it for a second marriage, to the same man no less. She thought about the simple sheath she had worn the first time in the Las Vegas wedding chapel. No, she deserved this dress, and Devin deserved to see her in it. They were getting a second chance and a new beginning.

Five giddy women burst into the room interrupting her reverie. She didn't mind, though, loving their excitement for her and Dev.

They all wore street length green and red dresses, perfect for Christmas. She wished Cindy could be here, but she was blessed to have the other

Candy Canes. She had told them to choose a Christmas green or red dress, any style, one they might wear again. Just short, please. It was the new vogue to allow attendants to select their own dresses and not be burdened with some atrocity they would never wear again. Natalie and Doreen were the only ones who chose red because they said they hoped to be invited to a Valentine Day date. Theirs were both full-skirted, the hems flirting with their knees. Nat and Billy were an item now, so that date was almost a given. Doreen had somehow linked up with Bill Junior. Maybe Bill Senior had something to do with that. Two models together – imagine!

Melanie and Noelle wore slim, figure hugging green, and Connie wore one of her own designs in green, very understated so she wouldn't be over shadowing Candy. She was thrilled to have designed a special dress for Candy. After all, the girl hadn't had a proper wedding the first time. Connie, the social and creative one, couldn't imagine not having a wedding in style. Elopement! Ha!

Candy looked gorgeous, if Connie did say so herself. Her dress was almost ethereal. Even though the aisle was short, she would float down it on her brother Billy's arm.

The Candy Canes were escorted by Brad, Nick and Jeremy Cox, Devin's boss. Braydon escorted Noelle, and Bill Junior escorted Natalie who was Maid of Honor. The red and green theme was joyously Christmas.

Vivian wore a deep green sheath with a flirty little jacket, very becoming to her slim figure. Bill

CANDY'S WILD RIDE

Senior was honored to be Best Man. He not only had a daughter now, but soon he would have another son. The flowers, designed by Braydon, were all white with the barest of glittery green sprinkles on the petals. He adjusted his stephanotis boutonniere and green glitter stuck to his fingertips.

~

Devin stood stock still rigid, hands folded in front of him clasping the ring. He trusted Bill with the ring, but since it was the first and original one he had given to Candy, he wanted to hold it himself. It was a narrow ring with a tiny diamond, all he could afford at the time, and the one she had thrown at him in court. For Valentine Day he would give her another, big and glittery.

Music started to play. He wasn't sure why he and Bill were standing here in front of the pastor already. He realized he hadn't controlled his anxiousness. The music was supposed to have been their cue to take their places. But, Bill kindly followed his lead with a firm reassuring hand on his shoulder.

How interesting he thought for the umpteenth time that she had chosen to re-marry in New Hope, the church connected to the school where she worked. He knew it wasn't the church she went to every Sunday because he had started going to Mariners with her. But, Pastor Steve was special to her. His gentle voice suddenly started to greet everyone. It was almost a stage whisper, so intimate, just for the guests and God.

Pastor's wife, Patti, played the piano. No fancy organ or harp, just sweet music. Suddenly, the traditional wedding march sang from the piano keys. Did he have the strength to turn around and watch his bride walk down the aisle? Yes, he did.

He glanced at Pastor Steve. His smile was almost as wide as Devin's. That offered him enormous hope. Bill's hand gave Devin's arm a squeeze. They both turned to see a vision in loveliness drifting toward them.

Nobody noticed Miss Dana in the back of the church. She was grinning and dabbing her eyes. Another one of her teachers had found happiness. Little Aaron would be so glad.

THE END

ABOUT THE AUTHOR

Bonnie Engstrom and her psychologist husband, Dave, live in Arizona near four of their six grandchildren. The other two live in Costa Rica where they surf. The couple share their Arizona home with Sam and Lola, their two rescued mutts in charge of the household.

She used to bake dozens of Christmas cookies in November and freeze them so she would have a lot to pass out to neighbors. Now … well, that was a long time ago. Instead of cookies for Christmas, she writes. Her Candy Cane stories set in Newport Beach, California, where her family was raised and where they have many fond memories, are perfect for gift giving. Or, for just cuddling up by the fire for an inspiring romance read. She hopes you enjoy Her Wild Ride and also gift it to a special female in your life. Don't forget to leave an honest review on Amazon.

www.ingramcontent.com/pod-product-compliance
Lightning Source LLC
LaVergne TN
LVHW010333070526
838199LV00065B/5732